"In these stories in this co[...] once that he is in the presence of a consummate craftsman. Lawrence worked on many of these stories for years, even for decades. The sentences have a particular kind of balance and weight, and they have a rigor, too. Everything extraneous has been stripped away. Try reading them aloud, and you'll see how naturally they blend with one another, how effortlessly they convey a movement of thought and imagination. Distilled down to their essence, they have a depth, a richness, an integrity, and a character of their own. These sentences are the perfectly sawn pieces, each of them with its own grain and facets, that Lawrence has assembled in these stories."

—Stephen Goodwin, professor at George Mason University, author of *Breaking Her Fall*, *The Blood of Paradise*, and *Kin*

"Lawrence Reynolds is one of the most exceptional people I have ever met. His short stories are excellent."

—Robert Watson, author of *A Paper Horse*, *Advantages of Dark*, *Christmas in Las Vegas*, *Selected Poems*, *Night Blooming Cactus*, *The Pendulum*, *Three Sides of the Mirror*, *A Novel*, Pulitzer Prize Runner-Up for *Advantages of Dark*

"Following in the lineage of his mentor, Peter Taylor, Reynolds' unique voice in this collection offers a penetrating yet deceptively simple glimpse into a quirky slice of Americana, a long-forgotten time and place that comes alive through his masterful, unembellished craft and clarity of observation."

—Eliezer Sobel, author, *Minyan: Ten Jewish Men in a World That is Heartbroken*

"Lawrence Reynolds possesses one of most sensitive and original minds I have ever been in touch with."

—Peter Taylor, author of *A Summons to Memphis*, Pulitzer Prize winner for fiction

"Lawrence Reynolds lives his life thoughtfully, lovingly, and with zest. His stories reflect these characteristics and more. His elegantly-simple prose has the sparkle of good poetry that expresses the wisdom—and humor—of an ageless Virginia. This book is a deeply satisfying read."

—Larry Kinney, Ph.D., energy efficiency researcher

West of Phoebe

West of Phoebe

Stories by
Lawrence Judson Reynolds

RAINBOW RIDGE
BOOKS

Some of these stories first appeared in the following:
*The Greensboro Review, Christopher Street, Blackbird,
Cutthroat, Intro I, Richmond Quarterly Review
of Literature* and *The Greensboro Reader.*
"Proceedings" was adapted for the stage and presented
as a dramatic piece by the Green Alley Theater Company
in 1980 at the Empire Theatre in Richmond Virginia

Cover and interior design by Frame25 Productions
Cover photo © ESB Professional c/o Shutterstock.com

Published by:
Rainbow Ridge Books, LLC
140 Rainbow Ridge Road
Faber, Virginia 22938
www.rainbowridgebooks.com
434-361-1723

If you are unable to order this book from your local
bookseller, you may order directly from the distributor.

Square One Publishers, Inc.
115 Herricks RoadGarden City Park, NY 11040
Phone: (516) 535-2010
Fax: (516) 535-2014
Toll-free: 877-900-BOOK

Library of Congress Cataloging-in-Publication Data applied for.

ISBN 978-1-937907-50-1

10 9 8 7 6 5 4 3 2 1

Printed on acid-free recycled paper
in the United States of America

Table of Contents

Preface by Fred Chappell   xiii

Introduction   xv

1. The Man with the Gun   1

2. A Family Tree   23

3. My Father's Necktie   43

4. Proceedings   81

5. That Grand Canyon   103

6. The Half-Life of Holidays   127

7. Early Dylan: Five and Ten Cent Women   135

8. Last of the June Apples   165

About the Author   187

This book is dedicated to the one I love,

Margaret Ann Halsted Reynolds

Special thanks are due to everyone I've ever known
or imagined or dreamed of, especially the characters in
my stories who carry on when my imagination falls short.

Brothers

Preface

The Lonesome Community
of Lawrence Reynolds

by Fred Chappell

The eight stories that make up *West of Phoebe* by Lawrence Reynolds combine to form a portrait of a place and time in our American experience so familiar that they have become strange. It is as if the daily landscape we know so well, each of us separately and together, were presented in the guise of photographs taken with old Kodaks, or even ancient Brownie box cameras. Familiar but strange—sometimes even spooky:

Was the man with the gun actually there? How did the father's necktie change into a snake and then into the tail of a kite seeking its freedom in infinity? Is the ambiguous relationship of Raymond Miles and Emmitt Kinds, as revealed in "Proceedings," describable in words, or is its mystery its whole meaning? Is that relationship, of attraction and repulsion simultaneously, analogous to the one between the storeowner and the man who had robbed her fifty years earlier?

None of the mystery that pervades these stories wafts into them from the universe of fantasy. Reynolds presents his narratives in straightforward, nearly deadpan, fashion. Even his confused, daydreaming teenagers report their experiences in closely factual, personally reportorial, manner. They tell us what they see and when they tell us what they feel, omitting no flush of embarrassment, we know that they describe just what they have observed within and about themselves.

All these stories center upon single individuals and sometimes, as in "That Grand Canyon," upon a single scene. But the characters' isolated, tightly knit communities are present with them always. Each place they inhabit, the animals they live with, even the inanimate objects they touch possess histories, and none of them, not even outliers like Dalton Dean, in "The Last of the June Apples," can be separated from the histories. Sherwood Anderson and Thornton Wilder had the ability to draw a collocation of loners into an emotional community. Reynolds shares that talent.

That grand storywriter Peter Taylor once told me in private conversation that Mr. Reynolds' stories had "quiet power." When I tried to pursue the subject he purposely drifted from it, as if he too found it difficult to speak precisely about these natural, preternatural fictions.

To salute, as now I do, the fine and unique achievement of Lawrence Reynolds brings me a large and overdue happiness.

Introduction

Route 460 runs through the mythical village of Phoebe. At least it did when I was young, when these stories were first sketched in my imagination. Since then the highway has been moved and a new bypass has taken its place and a piece of history is lost. No matter. History is not really history. You cannot make history from what little we know. You cannot tell the truth with words.

Yet we keep trying. We try to tell the truth about our past. Where we lived. The heartbreak of our love. The cruelty of our master. The whisper of wind through a field of corn. The scorn of people we thought we knew. The depth of our despair. The vastness of our ego.

It's true that I thought I could find the true story of my father, who died when I was nine years old, if I just uncovered every clue, but the truth is large and stretches from here to there with no beginning and no end.

The stories in this book are not meant to be true. I hope they carry some truth in them. They are a part of my history.

The Man with the Gun

The highway was our river, linking backwater towns and villages like Phoebe to the great world. In earlier times it was called the "Richmond Turnpike," but in my childhood it was always referred to as "four-sixty," not Route 460, or U.S. Highway 460 (its official designation), but simply "four-sixty." In 1944, when I was three, my father opened a country store on four-sixty about a mile west of the village of Phoebe. Four-sixty ran through the heart of Virginia from the ocean to the mountains but during the war years, it was little more than a country road.

Even then, I could feel its possibilities, its promises, its disappointments this road would one day bring me.

Ours was a community of family farms. I have a few vague memories of those years: old men working with horses in the fields. My mother cooking on a woodstove and saving bacon grease to make lye soap. And worry. Every family had someone in the service to worry about and wonder if they would ever come home.

But in that time of rationed gasoline the highway carried only a hint of what was to come. By day, tractor-trailers,
delivery trucks, and cars drifted by randomly. Often there
were long gaps when the road was empty. It was a black
hard-surfaced road, shiny as a snake. The only sustained
flow of traffic was the convoys of Army trucks hauling men
and equipment to Norfolk. In the evening the road spread
its darkness around us, buoyed us up to drift through the
long night under a lace curtain of stars.

On those rare occasions when a brave traveler ventured
onto the nocturnal road, we could see the headlights a mile
away, rising like swamp gas, growing larger and larger, until
the vehicle flickered past our store, whipping shadows
through the dark room where my brother and I slept.

It was not light but the absence of light that woke me
one night soon after we moved there. It is one of my ear-
liest memories. I woke to the sound of engines rumbling
along the highway—not one engine but many—passing one
after another. I sat up in bed and stared at the dark window. There was no light, just the drone of engines going on
and on and on. Occasionally I thought I saw a ripple in the
darkness the way water roils up when something swims just
beneath the surface . . . but there was nothing I could actually see. At first I was too frightened to move, but gradually
the sound became calming and rhythmic. My brother was
asleep in the bed beside me. In the room next to ours my
mother was sleeping . . . and my father. I put my head back
down on the pillow and thought of my father, this small,
quiet stranger who had just come into my life. Was he

asleep beside my mother, or was he out there on the highway? Was he going away again? One part of me would be happy to have him gone, but another cried out for him not to leave. The engines droned on and on and I fell asleep and dreamed. In my dream the highway became a serpent, shiny and black, slithering through the fields and forest, no head, no tail, just a body swelling like a river about to flood.

A country store was what our place became, although I have always believed my father had something more in mind when he bought it. Previous owners had operated a number of businesses there. The main building, which became our store and our home, had been a restaurant; booths still lined the walls in the front room. There were "tourist cabins," four of them stretched out along the highway (two on either side of the store) and a garage, actually an old tobacco barn converted to a garage. My father had been a mechanic before he married, but my mother did not want him to return to that profession.

Did my father envision the booming tourist business that would come after the war, with thousands of new cars rolling out of Detroit and people driving around the country just for the fun of it? They would need a place to eat, a place to sleep, maybe even a little entertainment. What dreams did he have for this plot of ground that would, one day, become my center of the universe? I'll never know.

I have few memories of those years. My father is long since dead but I feel I know him better every day. He was thirty-seven when he married my mother. What he did for those first thirty-seven years and why he stayed unmarried

3

for so long I have never discovered. It must have been difficult for him becoming a husband and father at that age. My mother has always been tight-lipped on the subject but I have heard rumors over the years.

When the war came he was forty-two with another child (me) just born. All the young men were leaving to go to war. I imagine him brooding, as I sometimes do, over missed opportunities. It was then he left us and went to work in the Tidewater area, where the Chesapeake Bay empties into the Atlantic. This was an important military area. Jobs were plentiful. Norfolk, Newport News, Portsmouth were all booming.

Of course it wasn't called a separation in those days and there was the excuse of working in the "war effort," as my mother always called it. What he did in the war effort I do not know. When I was young I believed he worked in the Naval shipyard—I am not sure why, perhaps my mother led me to believe this. Several years after he died, someone told me, jokingly perhaps, that my father ran a bar in Portsmouth during the war. But I am not sure either is true. He never spoke of that time and my mother now says she is not sure what he did.

He was only four hours away but for three years he did not come home. The gas shortage was blamed. We lived with mother's people on the farm. Our mother reminded us every night that we had a father "working in the war effort." Our grandparents seldom mentioned him. I do not remember that he wrote to us but years later I found a note in a Methodist hymnal that belonged to my mother—faded ink on blue paper, surprisingly feminine: "Dearest E, This is for the boys' Christmas things and for you. Buy yourself something pretty." There was no date and no signature, yet I will always believe this was a letter from my father written during that period of separation. There was also a postscript written at the bottom of the page: "Remember me to Winnie."

I regret now that I did not take the note, for later it disappeared from the book and I have never seen it again. Once I asked mother who Winnie was, whom she and father had apparently known when they were first married. My mother has always been an honest woman without a drop of deceit in her blood; yet, I felt she lied when she said that there was no one named Winnie whom she could recall.

Was Winnie a man or a woman? Why was this message written as a postscript when there was no signature? It was definitely intended as a separate and distinct message apart from the business of Christmas gifts for "the boys" (I note that we are not named) and the touches of affection (Dearest . . . Buy yourself something pretty.) I sometimes imagine that the body of the letter, and even the money enclosed, were merely covers for the real message —"Remember me to Winnie." But why I think so, I am not sure.

⊂#⊃

The tourist cabins were small, white-frame structures with metal roofs painted red. On the side facing the highway, a message was painted on each cabin, meant to be read in succession, like a Burma-Shave sign:

TOURIST AND TRAVELLER
FROM WHEREVER YOU ROAM
EAT AND SLEEP WITH
COMFORTS OF HOME

The original builder had intended, I believe, to fulfill this promise. Each cabin was built with its own bathroom— a tiny room with a sink and a toilet. However no plumbing had ever been installed. When we moved there, the only plumbing on the entire place was a single water line that ran from the well house to our kitchen. Our house—which consisted of the back three rooms of the store—had no bathroom either although my father added one soon after we moved there. What happened to the good intentions of the original builder of these cabins I do not know. I sus- pect they must have been built in the `20s when someone like my father had dreams of a highway filled with tourists before the crash and the great depression that followed.

Apparently the lack of plumbing had not proved an obstacle to their use. As a child I and my brother explored them in a way only children can. We looked in every corner, on every shelf, under the mattresses of the beds that were left there, in the dresser drawers, and behind the mirrors. The signs of life were abundant—old newspapers, combs, hairpins, lipstick tubes, a small cigarette lighter made in the shape of a Coca Cola bottle. But what my brother found in one of the cabins sparked our imagination more than any-thing else. It was the casing of a .32 caliber bullet, its brass still shiny as new. Later, my brother showed me what he said was a bullet hole in the plaster wall above the bed. We searched the floor for bloodstains, but my brother finally decided they had wiped the blood up before it dried.

Soon after we moved in my father turned one of the cab-ins into his "office." By day he went about the business of set-ting up a general store. He built shelves and counters, met with salesmen, nailed signs to the sides of the building adver-tising Royal Crown Cola, Nehi, Lucky Strikes, and Chester-fields. In the evenings, he worked in the cabin on his plans. What those plans were I do not know. No record of them survives, and to be honest, I am not sure they were ever actu-ally written down. (He was not a man much given to writ-ing.) But I knew even then that these plans were important to him. He worked on them late into the night. Sometimes when he came in from working my brother and I would wake to whispered arguments between him and my mother.

My brother, who was six at the time, remembers that my father wanted to reopen the restaurant and my mother did not. I can certainly believe that my mother would have objected to such a plan—even today she is contemptuous of "eating out," as if it were somehow sinful. In her mind she sees restaurants as only one step removed from cafes, taverns, bars—places of strong drink and questionable behavior. She would have had nothing to do with running such an establishment, especially one that was virtually the front room of her home.

Still, as my father stocked the shelves of the store and installed the drink box, the scales and the cash register, he did not remove the booths that lined the wall. Once we opened for business, some of our customers would take drinks from the drink box and sit in the booths and drink them. After a few months, Curley Orndolf, with his crew of pulpwood cutters, began coming by almost every day. They sat in the booths and ate sardines and crackers. The smell drifted through the house and the cracker crumbs littered the floor. I don't remember my mother ever actually saying anything but I could feel her displeasure. By our second year there, the booths were gone.

One summer day during the first year we lived there my brother and I were sitting in the side yard. It was late morning and pleasantly hot, not sticky hot the way July and August would be, so it must have been June. My brother was out of school for the summer and we were barefooted and each day stretched out lazily before us. This day promised to be a day like many others until I became aware of the stillness of the highway. It was as if someone had thrown a dam across the river and cut off the flow. The highway was silent but in that silence it seemed to be saying something to me, something I could not understand, but something that kept me looking out to the road every chance I got.

My brother was teaching me to shoot marbles. In a bare spot in the yard he drew a circle in the dirt and put the marbles in the center then shot them with his steely—a shiny ball bearing he had found in the old garage. My brother was a great marble shooter. He had a quart jar full of marbles he had won at school that year, but now it was summer and he was bored. He wanted competition but I offered none. My hands were too small to hold a marble in the proper shooting position. His steely was smaller and might have worked well in my little fist but it was his prized possession and there was no way I would be allowed to use it.

After a while he gave up on me and played a make-believe game with himself. I watched in admiration as the silver steely, fired by his thumb, shot across the ground and exploded the tightly bunched marbles. Two or three rolled outside the circle. Then, one by one he shot the other marbles out, putting English on the steely so that it stopped within the circle. His was a skill I would never master, but at the time I didn't know that.

As I sat watching my brother and also keeping an eye on the highway, a man appeared on the silent road. It was not unusual to see people walking along the highway in those days. Gas was still in short supply and people used the edge of the highway as a footpath. Many of our customers walked to our store, or sent their children. There were several hobos who walked the road on a regular basis, picking up drink bottles and selling them to my father for two cents apiece. Once a column of soldiers passed, marching in single file, though we never found out where they came from or where they were going—the nearest military installation was Camp Pickett, fifty miles away. But the man I saw that day was different. He was not a neighbor or customer or hobo or a soldier. He was not like anyone I had ever seen before. He walked just on the edge of the pavement and he seemed to move with purpose as if he knew exactly where he was going and what he was going to do when he got there.

When I first saw him he had already passed in front of our store, heading west on the highway. As he came abreast of the first tourist cabin he stepped off the pavement, walked a few steps along the shoulder of the road, then stepped across the ditch and disappeared behind the cabin. He never broke stride, as if this were a natural path for him that he had walked many times before.

My brother finished his game of marbles. His back was to the road and he did not see the man. I did not say anything and he began collecting his marbles from the grass and putting them back in the circle. I waited for the man to appear on the other side of the cabin but he did not. It was mid-morning. The sun was high above us. I could hear my father hammering in the store as he built more shelves. Earlier, my mother had come to the kitchen door and thrown out a pan of dishwater. Now robins scratched in the wet dirt, pecking at scraps of food. The silence of the highway was broken suddenly as three cars sped by in quick succession. They were all police cars. There were no flashing lights or sirens, just the sound of their tires on the pavement. The sound seemed to whisper: "Strange. Strange. Strange."

The man had not reappeared from behind the cabin and I was beginning to wonder if this was all a dream. My brother often accused me of making things up. But those things were real to me; I just couldn't prove that they were. Later I was told that these were dreams, that they hadn't really happened. Once I accepted this explanation these experiences, all of which involved the highway, stopped. But I know they were not dreams.

With the marbles bunched in the circle again, my brother loaded the steely in his fist and took aim. But this time he fired with such force the steely never touched the ground. It hit the marbles a glancing blow and ricocheted into the high grass.

"Darn!" he said.

He began searching in the grass but he was nowhere near the steely. I had seen exactly where it landed but I did not say anything. I was afraid my vision of the flight of the steely might have been too good, that it might be one of my dreams.

"Darn!" he said again as he grew more frantic. He knew better than to say "damn." My mother did not allow cursing. I always assumed my father agreed but years later I was told by an old friend of his that he could "cuss keen as a gnat."

I could see the steely shining in the grass a good distance from where my brother was looking, but I wasn't really interested. I was still waiting for the man to reappear from behind the cabin. I was beginning to be worried that this was a dream I wanted out of.

Finally I said—not so much to my brother as to myself: "There's a man behind the cabin."

My brother began patting the grass, then tearing at it with his fingers. I didn't think he heard me. So I said it again because now I wanted him to hear me:

"There's a man . . ."

"What man?" he shouted.

"... behind the cabin. He went behind the cabin and didn't come out."

"Who cares? It's just Uncle John or somebody. Help me find my steely. Darn!"

"It's not Uncle John," I said.

Uncle John was not our uncle. He was the farmer who owned the land that surrounded our store but from the very first he said we should call him uncle and we always did.

"It's not anyone we know," I said.

My brother is a mild-mannered person, slow to anger, and not given to frustration, but this— combined with his lost steely—sent him into a rage. He hit the ground with his fists and yelled at me.

"Then who the hell is it?"

I looked around to see if my mother was listening. I knew "hell" was one of the words we weren't supposed to say. But no one was around. There were only the two of us. But a voice said to me: "No, the three of us." It was true; behind the tourist cabin there was a third person. I didn't know who it was but I suddenly had a strong premonition.

"I think he lives here," I said. I had no idea why I said that. Perhaps it was because he'd seemed so at home, walking the way he had. After I said it I felt a bit frightened.

My brother was even more incensed.

"You're crazy. Nobody lives here but us."

He was right of course. Nobody lived there but us. We didn't even offer the tourist cabins for rent. But the man I had seen looked like he lived there. He looked at home.

Maybe, I thought, more at home than we did. But how could I explain that to my brother?

"What about the bullet?"

"What bullet?"

"The bullet you found in the cabin."

My brother's face took on a look of superiority.

"That was before, stupid . . . before we moved here. He doesn't live here now. He's long gone."

"I think he's back," I said.

"Who's back?"

"The man with the gun."

For the first time my brother seemed interested.

"You saw a man with a gun?"

"No, but it looked like him."

"Like who?"

"The man with the gun."

My brother looked at me, a little angry, but I could also tell he was beginning to believe me.

"You're crazy," he said.

For the moment he had stopped thinking about his lost steely. A tractor-trailer roared past heading toward Lynchburg, then several cars came by in quick succession. We were quiet until the hissing sound of their tires faded into the distance. Then it seemed unnaturally quiet.

"He's behind the cabin," I whispered because it occurred to me for the first time that the man might be listening to everything we said.

My brother looked toward the first cabin and I nodded my head. This was indeed the cabin where he had found the bullet and the bullet hole.

It is seldom that the younger brother has the upper hand but in this instance I clearly felt I had power over my brother. Therefore it was incumbent upon me to do something, to take the lead. I got up and motioned for him to follow me. We slipped behind the hedgerow at the back of the yard, made our way through the grape arbor, and dashed across an open space until we were safely hidden behind the big garage. By looking around the corner of the garage we would be able to see between the cabins where the man had disappeared.

I crept along the back wall until I reached the corner. But I was afraid to look. What if I looked right into his eyes? What if he were standing just around the corner? What if he had a gun? The power I had felt left me. I stood with my back flat against the wall. I couldn't move.

Finally, my brother pulled me back and inched toward the corner himself. But he stopped short of actually looking and I knew he too was afraid.

From the back of the garage I could see across the rolling fields of Uncle John's farm. There were rows of corn and rows of tobacco. And beyond the fields were trees and a lane that led to Uncle John's house and behind the house—on the other side of Hagg's Creek—was the beginning of the big forest that reached to the top of Pilot Mountain. The whole world seemed to be quiet and I could hear my own breathing. I had been afraid in the dark before, but never like this, in the middle of the day, in the bright sunlight.

We might have stayed frozen there till sundown except for the passing of a Greyhound bus on the highway. People often caught the bus to Lynchburg in front of our store. As it came up the hill the bus driver would blow his horn to give warning to anyone who might be waiting inside the store. If no one came out, he would roar on away without stopping.

The sound of the bus horn seemed to break the spell of fear we were under. I saw my brother crouch down, then lie down on his belly. With his elbows he began to crawl forward to the corner of the garage. This seemed like a safe way to take a look without being seen. I got down and started to crawl up beside him but he waved me back.

"What do you see?" I whispered.

He hadn't seen anything yet because he hadn't looked. Finally, keeping his head low to the ground, he pulled himself forward and peered around the garage.

"Do you see him?" I whispered.

He turned back to me and raised his fist.

"What'd you see?"

"Nothing. There's nobody behind the cabin. You made it up."

"Nobody?"

"Nobody! Nothing! You made it up. You're always making stuff up in your head."

I couldn't believe it. Where could he have gone? I looked around the corner of the garage myself but he was right. There was nothing. Just a space between the cabins where you could see out to the highway.

"He's gone."

"He wasn't ever there. You made it up."

He was mad because I had frightened him. Whatever power I had was gone. I was the little brother again.

I looked around the corner of the garage again. Nothing. Had I been dreaming? It all had seemed so real. He was walking on the pavement when I first saw him, then on the shoulder, then he stepped across the ditch and walked behind the cabin. I could still remember what he looked like—short and thin with dark hair. He was wearing dark pants and a white shirt. The cuffs of the shirt were rolled over once and on his left arm, above the elbow, he wore a dark armband. He was not a man I had ever seen before, nor was he like anyone I had ever seen before, but he was too real to be a dream.

If he wasn't a dream, he had to be somewhere. Then I remembered how deliberately he walked, as if he knew exactly where he was going, as if he lived here. Of course . . . it suddenly occurred to me . . . of course he wouldn't be standing behind the cabin. No. He would be in the cabin.

The doors to all the cabins were on the side away from the store. The screen door to the first cabin was closed but the inside door was open. I ducked back behind the garage.

"He's in the cabin," I whispered.

"You must think I'm stupid; you think I'd fall for this again?" my brother shouted at me.

I signaled for him to keep his voice down.

"The door's open."

"So?"

"It was closed this morning."

My brother looked again.

"So what? I'll bet there's nobody in there."

"I know he's in there," I said, "it's the only place he could be."

"The only place he could be is in your stupid head. Come on, I'll show you."

He grabbed my arm and pulled me toward the cabin. I pretended to hold back but I really wanted to see if he was in there so I let myself be pulled along.

Even before we got to the door I heard the sound and knew I was right. It was a sound like blowing bubbles in your milk, that, and then another sound like the sound I made when I tried to whistle.

In the bright sunlight we could not see through the screen door, but when we moved into the shadow of the cabin my brother froze. At first we could only see the arm of a white shirt hanging off the bed, the cuff rolled over once. Then we could make out the hand hanging from the sleeve. Finally the whole picture came into focus. The man was stretched out on the bed, his arm hanging down, almost touching the floor. He was snoring.

"Who is it?" my brother whispered. Suddenly he seemed to think I knew something that he didn't.

We stood just outside the door of the cabin, afraid but too fascinated to run. The man went on snoring as we stared at him. He was not one of our neighbors, I could tell that when I first saw him. His white shirt and black pants were not exactly church clothes but they were definitely not what men in our community wore to work. He was a small man with curly black hair, worn longer than men wore their hair then. The white shirt he wore was wrinkled. But what I remember most distinctly about him was the way he slept, so soundly it might have been the middle of the night. I don't believe I had ever before seen a man asleep in the middle of the day. My grandfather sometimes napped after his noonday meal, which we called dinner, but that was not serious sleep. This man was asleep at noon, in a strange bed, as if it were the middle of the night.

The other thing I remember was that I was not afraid of him. He might have been the man with the gun—he might have had a gun on him at that very moment—but he did not seem like someone who would hurt you.

Apparently my brother did not share this feeling. As soon as he got a good look at the man, he turned and ran around the corner of the cabin leaving me there still staring through the screen door. I knew he was off to get our father and for some reason I wished he wouldn't.

At that moment I became aware that the snoring had stopped. In the dim room an eye opened. It stared back at me. Still I was not afraid, only curious, and curious to know if he was indeed the man who had fired the bullet in the cabin. He seemed very much at home and the fact that I was staring at him did not seem to annoy him, as if he had lived a long time without privacy.

He raised himself up on an elbow, still looking at me, and reached for a pack of Camels that was on the night table.

"Where's Clara, kid?" He took a Camel from the pack, tapped it on his thumbnail, and put it in his mouth. "She still lives here, don't she?"

There was no traffic on the highway, and in the quiet I had heard him very plainly though he spoke in a low throaty voice. But what was he talking about? Who was Clara? Who was he? I knew he was waiting for an answer from me, but what came to my lips was a question.

"Do you . . . do you have a gun?"

I heard the screen door on the back porch of our house slam shut and I knew my father was on his way.

The man lit his cigarette. He answered as if it was the most natural question in the world.

"Naw, they took my gun along with everything else."

My father came around the corner of the cabin then and with one wave of his hand he sent me scurrying back to the kitchen where my mother and brother were waiting. As I passed through the side yard, I saw my brother's steely lying in the grass. I picked it up. It was round and smooth and cool to the touch. It was not fair that my brother played marbles so well and I played so poorly. It was not fair that he had a steely and I didn't. Yet I had seen the man with the gun. I had looked him in the eye and talked to him while my brother was hiding in the kitchen. I closed my fingers around the steely and put my thumb behind it in shooting position. I could hear the sharp crack as the steely attacked the marbles and I could see them scatter in the dirt like so many frightened fantasies of my youth.

When I got to the back steps I put my fist down on the open end of the length of galvanized pipe that was our handrail post and fired the steely into the pipe. It made a ringing sound as it spiraled its way down to its final resting place at the dark end of the pipe.

Years later, when they tore down the old store so the highway could be widened, I remembered the steely and looked through the rubble hoping I might find it still in the pipe, but like so much else from that time, it was not to be found.

Eventually, my brother found another steely and continued his reign as the marble-shooting king. He even gave some of them to me when he outgrew the game. But I was never any good. Perhaps my fingers were too stubby. Or perhaps I never had the concentration of my brother. I was too often dreaming, feeling the pull of the highway going east and west, imagining the lives of the strangers who passed so close to our doorway, but seldom stopped. My father had been right. The traffic picked up after the war. The road was filled with flashy new cars, and the cars were filled with people who ate at restaurants and stayed the night in motels. But they were not a part of our lives. My father went less and less often to his office. He spent his waking hours in the dark store, which in those early years seemed to me a forbidden place. Now fifty years later, I have a recurring dream. In the dream I see my father's silhouette in a doorway. He is staring out at the highway, the smoke from his cigarette rises in the sunlit frame and the cars flash by like ripples in a stream.

I don't know why, but I have never to this day told my brother what happened to his first steely, though in recent years we have talked frequently about the "man with the gun" (as we have always called him) and other things that happened at the store when we were children. Nor can I explain why I did such a thing to my brother, other than to say I had met an outlaw, I had looked him in the eye, I had spoken to him, and found myself perhaps to be not unlike him.

A Family Tree

(In memory of Charlie B. and
Sam I., who fought in the Good War)

There were four of them. Four huge oaks standing on the knoll surrounded by the clean, contoured fields and rolling pasture. The road along which Russell Cross walked curved gently up the knoll to where the trees stood against the setting sun.

There had been two at the front of the house and two at the back. With the house gone and the limbs on one side of each of the oaks seared to black sticks, the distance between the trees seemed greater than before. "Fifteen steps from each corner of the house," Aunt Vicky had maintained. For some reason, unknown even to Aunt Vicky, three of them were white oaks and one a pin oak. All that Russell Cross knew of the trees was that they had been there for as long as he could remember. He had climbed them years ago as a boy and they seemed no less huge then than now. From any window in the house you could see at least one of them. In the winter they shredded the wind and broke its impact. In the summer the house stayed cool in their dark blot of shade.

If Aunt Vicky's facts were right—and there was no reason to believe otherwise considering how much of her time she had given to studying the Cross family history—Russell's great-grandfather had built the house in 1858. "Crossroads" he had called his farm, commemorating the family name and the two roads that intersected about a mile from where the house stood. Aunt Vicky was proud to point out that "Crossroads" was still shown on the map, although the intersection was no longer a part of the farm. The original farm had been whittled down from over a thousand acres to the present two hundred acres where the old Cross house had stood. The old house had been Russell's home until Wednesday, a week ago, when a short in some wiring touched off a fire that burned it to the ground.

Walking along the road that led up to the house and thinking of Aunt Vicky who had been dead for over two years now, Russell was ashamed that he did not miss the house more. He had spent his whole life there except for the two-and-a-half years he had been in the army, yet he did not really miss it.

He and Carrie and the youngest of their six sons (the only one still living at home) were comfortable enough in a trailer out by the public road. "Boxes," he had always called them, but living in a trailer wasn't so bad. It was small but efficient. Everything worked properly. There were two front doors but no back door. It would take him awhile to get used to that.

They were lucky to have escaped the fire and to be set up in another home so soon. All his older boys and their families lived close by, and they helped. They all had jobs now, but they still worked with him on the farm when they could. They were, as Aunt Vicky always said, a credit to him. Now that he was settled in the trailer things were getting back to normal, but there was one last thing to be done at the old house.

He looked at its remains, a pile of grey ash and rubble lying between two stark chimneys. He had meant to come back sooner but there hadn't been time. There wasn't time today either, but he had left the boys in the hayfield and come in early to make his last search. If he found what he was looking for, he would get on with the business of farming again and maybe the dream would go away.

He stood at the right corner of the house and remembered the way the rooms had been laid out. What he was looking for was in the bureau drawer in the upstairs front bedroom, but after the fire there was no telling where it had ended up. It was only a heart-shaped medal with a piece of colored ribbon attached to it. It lay in a box lined with blue velvet. The box and the ribbon would have burned, but the medal he hoped would remain. It was the medal they had given him after the war, thirty-odd years ago.

He stepped over the foundation and pulled at a rusting sheet of tin that curled out of the ashes. The crust of ash formed by Sunday's rain rolled back and the dry ashes underneath bellowed up and settled on the legs of his overalls and the cracked tops of his work shoes.

With the tin he cordoned off an area about the size of the upstairs front bedroom. Then with a stick he scratched an outline of each piece of furniture: the bed, the dresser, the wardrobe, the bureau.

It was a childish way to begin but he could think of no other way to put things in perspective and start the search. He could not sift through every inch of the ashes and he wanted to feel that he was beginning at the point where the medal was most likely to be found.

He knelt down and began probing with a stick the area he had outlined for the bureau. Charred and melted pieces of glass and metal surfaced. Russell examined each one carefully and threw it aside.

In the hollow beside the house he heard the familiar sound of his old John Deere tractor. The boys were loading the last load of hay. It was already past suppertime. They had their own families to think of—the five oldest did. The least he could do was go back and help them. There was no time for a grown man to be scratching about in a pile of ashes for something he was not likely to find. Still, it had to be found. He knew that—felt it urgently at times, especially at night.

The dream had started again. Perhaps it was the sight of the flames from the house whipping into the night sky that had brought it back. It was the same dream that he had many times years ago, soon after the war. But over the years it had slowly faded. Now it came again, every night.

In the dream he and the German boy were swimming together in the ocean. They were swimming for pleasure—always it began that way. Side by side in the blue and the endless waters, they matched each other stroke for stroke. The German's eyes were as blue as the ocean. They met his eyes without fear. Stroke for stroke they swam. The rolling waves lulled them, denying them any sense of progress. They seemed to swim endlessly riding the crest and fall of the waves.

They swam faster, reaching their long arms out across the water, matching each other stroke for stroke, faster and faster. Then, somewhere in the depths of the German's eyes he saw a fear stirring. And in his own body he felt the fear he saw beginning there. Each stroke became compelled, giving rise to the next stroke. And the next.

But the pleasure remained. The pleasure of a hard fought race. But the fear was there too. The fear of losing. They swam harder and faster than before but still each matched the other perfectly, stroke for stroke.

Then in an instant the fear turned to panic. They lost all form, were breathless and exhausted, splashing and wallowing in the blue water. The panic he felt was the knowledge that one of them would drown. One of them would slip beneath the rolling surface of the water to be lost forever.

Then, just as he felt himself sinking, he would wake and the dream would end. But there was no real end to it. It always came again.

Years ago, when the dream was at its worst, Carrie would wake too.

"Russ?" she would say into the darkness that had so recently been a bright and vast ocean.

"Russell, it was a bad dream," she had said at first. But later when she knew him better, she only said his name, and put her arm about his waist and held him.

Russell dropped down on his hands and knees and dug vigorously. Putting aside the stick, he combed through the loose ashes with his fingers. A twisted metal picture frame surfaced and he held it up for a moment before throwing it aside.

It could have been any one of the three pictures that Carrie kept on the bureau. One was of his mother and father standing together in front of the house. Another was of him and Carrie standing in the same spot soon after they were married. The third was of his six sons and five grandsons taken just last year. ("Boys," Aunt Vicky had told Carrie after the second son was born, "run in the Cross family.")

There were other pictures in the house, stored away in the closets and the attic, that Russell remembered now. There was one in particular that sat on the mantel in the living room for awhile, years ago. In it, Russell stood in his uniform in front of a barracks at Fort Oglethorpe, Georgia. There was another soldier with him: a boy named Benson who was hamming it up for the camera while Russell stood erect and serious, almost at attention. They were just out of basic then. Their paths, Benson's and his, crossed several more times during the war. In England. In Africa. And again in England before the big landing.

In the years right after the war he often wondered what had happened to Benson. He wondered whether he had made it back. So many others that he had known had not.

But even before the picture came down from the mantel, he ceased having time to think about such things.

Russell spent a good part of his army life on the fringes of the war. After Oglethorpe, he was sent to England to await orders. Then to Africa where he served in a unit providing re-enforcements for the British. Then back to England without ever any real taste of fighting.

Then on an overcast morning in 1944 he found himself squatting in the metal belly of a landing craft churning over the rolling waves toward the shores of Normandy. There were no pictures of that part of his life, only the heart-shaped medal. The medal was not a picture of life. It was a life—a life he had kept alive though it had been dead thirty-odd years now.

⊂#⊃

The platoons of men squatted in lines on the wooden grate on the floor of the landing craft. They leaned against their rifles for balance and kept their helmeted heads low. The thud of each shell exploding in the water was like a hard punch in the stomach. Flames cracked in the sky but no one looked up.

Russell stared at a skim of grey water that drifted about in the bottom of the boat beneath the grating. It rushed toward the stern of the boat suddenly as the bow rose sharply. Each man shifted his weight against his weapon until the boat leveled again, came almost to a stop, then surged forward, its bow cutting into the water. A mist settled on them as the motors churned backwards slowing their approach. The men swayed, pushing their rifle butts hard against the floor grate. The trapped water slid back across the bottom of the boat.

A shell exploded on the beach before them, showering the boat with sand and in that moment the boat dug into the shoreline, tumbling the lines of men into one another. Then, as they struggled to their feet, the gate of the craft dropped open and they stared at the white beach and the dark hills of Normandy.

There was only one thing that Russell remembered of the landing: the softness of the sand and how slowly he ran in it.

Twelve thousand men died that day, but Russell could remember none of it. He could not remember firing his weapon. He remembered only the run. In the evening when his company regrouped he found that only half of the men from his boat had made it ashore. But he had not seen the others fall and die. It was as if they were bubbles that had burst and were gone forever.

He remembered moving forward again that night. But during the second day he lost all memory. They talked later of his bravery under fire, of how he had saved the life of a wounded man. But he remembered none of it. Somewhere during that day, he became separated from the advancing forces, and the next memory he had was a long and vivid one.

He was alone in a tangle of vines in a ravine. His head throbbed and his skull felt as thin as an eggshell. He rubbed his hands across his forehead and the dried blood flaked off like scales. A trickle of fresh, warm blood ran down his cheek.

The throbbing of the tractor motor made the memory of the pain real again and he lifted a finger dirty with ashes and touched the old scar on his forehead. In the field that ran along the creek in the back of the house the tractor emerged pulling a wagon piled high with hay.

He considered for a moment giving up his search and going to the barn to help his sons unload. But then his hand touched a small piece of metal in the ashes, and though it was not the metal he sought, his mind travelled back to the fields of Normandy and the time he had spent there alone.

The fields there were green, the way his own fields were today, yet they were different. From the vine-covered gully Russell could see a distant road bordered by a hedge-row. Through the break in the hedgerow he glimpsed a lone vehicle racing along the road. Far away, the sounds of war were like firecrackers exploding on the Fourth of July.

Russell crawled along the gully on his hands and knees. Occasionally he stopped and listened, but the war seemed to be fading into the distance. He crawled by instinct, not knowing where he was or where he was going, but keeping as close to the ground as possible.

His muscles ached yet he could not seem to relax them even when he stopped to rest. He felt cold and damp, yet his body burned as if with fever. More than anything he wanted a warm, safe place to sleep.

He crawled steadily along the gully until it merged with a small stream. The stream was a watering place for cattle.

Its sloping banks had given away to a muddy bog of hoof prints, yet there were no cattle to be seen. The hoof prints were old and filled with stagnant water.

Then Russell saw something that startled him. Across the creek, standing in a grove of trees, was a small white house. For a moment he felt calm and safe. It stood there as still and as pretty as a picture on a postcard.

Aunt Vicky used to say of Russell that he had "distinguished himself in the war." There were other Crosses who had distinguished themselves in other wars. There was Colonel Charles Clayton Cross who had fought with General Lee in "th' war." Aunt Vicky knew all the stories and told them with pride. But about Russell there were no stories. He had never told anyone. He felt no pride in having fought in the war. The war was something that caught him up, something that happened to him. He was not proud to have been so near death. He was not proud to have killed a man.

He was not proud of the medal they had given him. He kept it because it somehow held all that he could ever know of the German boy who swam with him through his sleep almost nightly, as if it were the boy's very life given to him to keep.

Russell dug deeper in the ashes. They stirred like wisps of smoke and settled on the hair of his wrists and forearms.

The area that he had drawn as the bureau was full of familiar objects: Carrie's iron, the curled sole of one of his work shoes, a six-inch bolt with a tap and three washers—the one he had used on the hitch of his tractor and brought home in his pants pocket by mistake the night of the fire. But there was no medal, only several heat-warped coins to give him false hopes.

After he finished the bureau area he rested for a moment and watched his sons putting the hay in the barn down near the creek. Then he began again, marking off a new area in front of the bureau and digging with the bolt he had found earlier.

There were ashes in the fireplace of the little house in Normandy but they had been cold for many days. Except for a pile of straw near the foot of the stairs, they were the only sign that the house had been occupied in recent years.

The thought of sleeping in the straw was tempting but Russell walked through it and cautiously crept up the steps. He wanted to be hidden, he wanted time to act if someone came into the house.

The second floor was one long, low room close to the thatched roof. A small window in the gable admitted a little light from the fading day. The room was empty.

It was just as well that Aunt Vicky was dead now, Russell thought as he dug through the ashes with the bolt. She would have taken the loss of the house very hard even though she owned no part of it. It was "home." "The home place."

She studied the past the way some people study the Bible. She could quote names and dates. She knew when the Crosses first settled in the county. She knew where the original log cabin had been built (in the middle of Russell's hayfield) and when it had burned. She loved to tell the story of a great-great uncle who had built a store at the intersection of the two roads. When the Yankees came through they asked for directions at the store and the old man sent them down the wrong road. She knew what had happened to the sons and grandsons and great grandsons and how the land had been divided among them and passed on, and how most of it eventually came to be sold to others.

She had always lived in Richmond, but in her later years especially, she came to visit them frequently. And though she called the old house "home" she always seemed out of place in it. Carrie, Russell knew, had always felt a little uncomfortable around her, as if what they had wasn't nice enough for Aunt Vicky.

Fortunately she spent most of her time when she came to visit at the county courthouse searching through the court records. She was making what she called a family tree. It was a large sheet of paper with the names of all the generations of Crosses. Though Russell had little interest in most of what Aunt Vicky did, he was fascinated by the family tree. It was sometimes hard for him to believe that all those people were a part of his family and that they had all descended from just two people way down at the bottom of the paper.

Aunt Vicky had shown Russell his own name high up in the branches of the tree and from his name six new branches had sprung. As he thought of it now, he could see himself pushed further down in the tree as the branches that sprang from him flourished with still more life. There were five grandchildren already. Soon there would be others.

He wondered what had become of the family tree. Aunt Vicky was dead now with no family living after her. The paper was probably thrown away when they cleaned out her apartment in Richmond. But the picture of the family tree lived on is Russell's mind. He often thought of it when he thought of the German boy whose branch he had forever severed.

Russell slept in a corner under the low, thatched roof, his arms curled about his weapon. He slept just on the edge of consciousness. Each time that his body began to relax into a deeper sleep his mind jerked him back again.

When the first glow of light came through the window he woke. He lay without breathing for a moment while his mind sought to recall where he was. He listened intently for sound, but there was none. Then, far away, he heard the cawing of a crow and it brought a memory to him which calmed him and started his breathing again.

In England he had learned that there was a bird like a crow that the English called a rook. At home they played a game called Rook. Sometimes on a hot Saturday night they would set up the card tables on the front porch of the old house and play until midnight. Almost everyone played. Sometimes there would be three or four games going at once. Russell's grandfather was a great lover of the game.

After each hand was dealt he would cry out: "Who's got the ol' bird this time?" And usually they could tell when he had it simply by the way he smiled when he asked the question.

Rook parties were a time for courting. Russell would ask Carrie over and the two of them would play partners. She wrote him now—letters from home. He carried them in the webbing of his helmet.

He sat up, holding his rifle to him. The sun would be up soon. He had to be out of the house and safely hidden before it was fully light. Perhaps, he thought, it had been a mistake to sleep in the house. A sudden fear came over him. A fear he could not explain. Had he heard something in the night, or had it only been a dream?

He slipped his finger over the trigger of his weapon and stood up. A board creaked beneath his weight and he stood up for a long time without moving. At last he started cautiously across the room, easing his weight from one foot to the other until he reached the stairwell. There he stopped and listened again. The stairwell was dark and the only sound was his own breathing and the heavy beating of his heart.

More than ever he felt that it had been a mistake to sleep in the house. The dawn was breaking rapidly and the silence with which it came was frightening. What if he were trapped on the stairs with nowhere to duck for cover?

He hesitated for a long time before putting his foot on the first, narrow step. The board sagged beneath his weight and he brought his other foot down quickly to the next step.

He descended several more steps before stopping short.

A square of light fell across the straw at the foot of the stairs and in the straw lay a hand, palm up. It was the hand of a German boy who lay asleep, sprawled on his back in the straw.

At first Russell could not see the boy, only the hand, and he aimed his rifle at it earnestly as if his only thought were to shoot it if so much as a finger moved.

The hand did not move and finally he descended another step. And another, until he could see the whole room and the sleeping body of the German who lay with his head against the landing just at the foot of the stairs, blocking Russell's way out of the house.

Stepping over him would be dangerous. His back would be turned. His advantage would be lost. He would be off-balance. What if his foot brushed the boy? What if the boards creaked and woke him? Even as he thought of stepping over him he knew there was no question of what he must do, and do immediately.

The rifle was still pointing at the boy's hand but he turned the muzzle now so that it was aimed at his head. The safety was unlocked though he could not remember unlocking it. All that was left to do was squeeze the trigger. Squeeeeze it, Cross, the sergeant used to whisper in his ear during basic training. Don't jerk it. Squeeeeze it.

But he did not squeeze it.

At first he could not, for there was no strength in his finger. Then as his courage returned he realized the danger of firing his weapon. In the silent morning the sound would travel for miles. Who knew how close the German's unit was? Were there other Germans within sight of the house even now?

He lowered the rifle slowly and his right hand went to his side where the bayonet hung in its sheath. Silently he withdrew it.

Now he stood awkwardly with a weapon in either hand. He was reluctant to set the rifle aside but he knew that he must. He needed to be free to act with one swift, decisive thrust.

A slight movement of the boy's arm made Russell start. He could not afford to have the boy wake now. He had to get rid of the rifle quickly. Without taking his eyes off the boy's face he set it quietly in the corner at the bottom of the stairs.

The boy slept on peacefully and Russell crouched over him with the bayonet raised. His thrust he knew must be swift and accurate. There would be no second chance. He had to silence the scream in the throat before it came.

He knew that death would not come instantly. The body would struggle. He had helped his father slaughter pigs. They would shoot them between the eyes and take them by the ears and run them about the yard until their legs buckled beneath them. A chicken's wings would beat like a hummingbird's when its head was chopped off and the blood would fly like rain.

Russell was not squeamish. He had seen the life go out of animals violently many times, yet the thought of plunging the bayonet into the sleeping boy made his blood go cold. He could not kill a man the way he killed a hog or a chicken.

For a moment he hesitated, thinking of his own life, praying that he might escape the house and find safety again in the vine-covered gully. Far away he could hear the crows again and closer by the house the twitter of other birds. The dawn was coming.

Although his eyes did not open the expression on the German's face seemed to change as if he sensed the danger hovering over him. Russell saw the change and reached quickly for his rifle. His fingers found the barrel and were about to close around it when it slipped from his grasp. He did not wait to hear it crash to the floor. He acted instinctively.

His eyes had never left the boy's face and as he dropped down beside him he pulled his chin back with his left hand and with his right he plunged the blade of the bayonet into the exposed throat.

Something seemed to crack as the blade entered. The German's eyes, so close to Russell's own, flew open and his face took on a shocked and stupid expression.

For an instant there was no blood. The wound was raw and white. Then the blood rose like coffee percolating in a pot, bubbling up about the knife blade and coming in great gulps as he lifted the blade.

The legs thrashed and the body rolled and a great sucking sound drew the blood inward, then blasted it out again like pellets from a blunderbuss, splattering Russell, splattering the walls, splattering the ceiling, with a torrent of blood-rain.

He was sweating, breathing heavily, plunging the bolt again and again into the soft floor of ashes when he found it, or what appeared to be it: a small piece of metal warped and melted beyond recognition.

He stood up, his hands and arms grey with ashes, and rubbed it with his thumb. But even before he did so he knew he would never be able to tell for sure if it were the medal. He rubbed it again and again, trying to know it from the touch, the feel of it.

The truth was that he did not know what was on the medal. He had never really looked at it or read its inscription. They had given it to him for bravery, but he thought of it only in relation to the German boy whose body he had left along with a match in the bloody straw.

When he ran from the house he forgot even to take his rifle. He ran along the creek bed, the water splashing wildly beneath his boots. The bayonet was still in his hand and he tossed it into the field as he ran. When at last he stopped running and looked back, the sun was rising through a haze of smoke that twisted from the roof of the little house.

He often wondered if anyone had ever found the body. He imagined someone, years later, cleaning up the debris and finding the bones. By then the boy would have been forgotten.

But Russell had not forgotten. He had kept the medal in memory of his life. Now, he had to admit, the medal too was gone forever.

He looked up at the huge oaks that surrounded him. A few blackened branches stood out against the sky. Next year there would be new leaves and still more the year after.

In a few years it would be hard to tell that there had ever been a fire.

He thought of Aunt Vicky's family tree. By now the German boy's tree had grown new life and buried him forever. Soon, Russell thought, he too would be lost in the growth of the great tree. He would be remembered for awhile by those who knew him. His sons and grandsons would remember him. But in time the memory would fade to make way for the living. The trouble with Aunt Vicky's tree was that it made no distinction between the living and the dead.

The German boy had been dead for many years and the medal could not change that. He would have to learn to deal with the dream differently. He had always known its ending. He was the victor—the living.

It was evening. In the shadow of the oaks it was almost dark. Russell rubbed the medal with his thumb once more, then dropped it back into the ashes. Far away he heard the shrill voice of his grandson calling him to supper. The tractor bolt was still in his hand, and considering that he might be able to use it again, he slipped it into the pocket of his overalls and turned back toward home.

My Father's Necktie

That was the summer I should have become a man. 1953. The year my father had a stroke. It was spring. Thornton and I got off the school bus at the edge of the highway and found the store closed, the door locked, the shades pulled down. A black Chrysler was parked in the driveway. It wasn't a car that belonged to anyone we knew. Something was wrong. Our father never closed the store during the day. Even when he was in his garage working on someone's car, the door was left unlocked, the shades up. If customers came they knew where to find him. If they were in a hurry they took what they needed and left money on the counter or a note telling him to put it on their account. That was the way country stores were. We walked around the side of the store to the house. Our mother was waiting. She herded us to the table on the side porch. We put our books on the table and sat down. I put my head back and looked up at the pale blue sky with its thin patches of gauzy clouds. It was a mild day with sudden gusts of wind that had a bite of cold in them. It would be a good day to fly a kite. I didn't have a kite, but that was no problem. I became a kite. I puffed myself up and waited for the next gust of wind to lift me. Then from high above I would look down on the store, the house, the garage, the highway as they grew small and insignificant.

I was waiting to be lifted up when I heard my mother say: "Your father's had a stroke."

A stroke? I knew what a stroke was. I had seen old people crippled by them. But when I heard the word come from my mother's lips that day all I could think of was the smooth motion of a hand stroking cat's fur. My father? A stroke? In my mind's eye I saw a hand caressing my father's head. There is a bald spot on the very top. The fingers are moving toward it. The hand thinks it is petting a cat. It is not expecting the slick, bald spot. The hand is in for a big surprise. I grin at my brother, but suddenly I'm aware of my brother's countenance. He's not smiling. He's looking at my mother. They seemed to share a sense of shock, sorrow, and determination while I am caught with an inappropriate grin on my face.

My father survived that first stroke and a second. He lived in his changed state for another six years but he was never the same. I remember very little about him after the stroke. It wasn't just his appearance—the lifeless half of his body, the drool slipping from the corner of his mouth, the desperate look in his good eye as it searched this limited universe for some relief from this new and awful reality. No, it wasn't the physical change that made me avoid him during those six years. It was the awful secret we shared from that summer that I had locked away in my memory for so long.

Thornton was fifteen, already working with the men in the fields and helping father with the store. Like father he was a quiet, competent worker. He could be "depended on." That's what the men, the farmers who were the main customers of our store, said about him. It was their highest praise. I thought I would be just like my brother when I became a man. I would no longer be a day-dreamer. I would no longer think or say or do "foolish" things. It was just a matter of time and the time was fast approaching.

I hid my mouth with my hand as our mother gave us our instructions. We were not to come into the house until she called us and we were to be very quiet. We could work on our homework on the porch. I could do my usual chores and Thornton could feed the Cantons' livestock as usual. Supper would be late. She would call us when it was ready. She said nothing about father's condition other than to say he was "resting" and a doctor from Lynchburg was with him. Then she went back inside.

Thornton opened one of his books and began his homework. I tried to do the same, but my thoughts wandered. I kept thinking about Thornton and how he had changed. In some ways I was like my brother. Everyone commented on how much we looked alike, how polite we were, how quiet and considerate we were. But I knew we were also very different. As children Thornton and I had been a team. He was the serious one. I was the joker, the jester, the rascal—the one that got us into trouble. Thornton was always there to rescue us. It was a natural role for me but now I was beginning to see that there was no place for foolishness in the world of men. Being a man was serious. I had only to look at Thornton. The change in him in the last two years had been amazing. To the adults it may have seemed merely an extension of his youthful self—serious, responsible, level-headed—the kind of boy you'd expect to grow easily into manhood. They didn't know him as I did. They didn't know that many of the roles I played as the fool were from scripts created by him. Now, he had given up childish things and moved into the world of men. It was no fun playing the fool alone.

I looked up from the pages of the book and studied the concentration on Thornton's face, the confidence. That's what I lacked. That's what I had to gain. I felt a weakness in the pit of my stomach. Somehow it didn't seem possible.

I sensed a slight movement in the corner of my eye and looked up to see a big chicken hawk drifting slowly in the evening sky in search of a meal. And just like that I found myself drifting on the wind, daydreaming, while my father lay in a coma just inside the closed door. How much easier it was to be a hawk than to be a man.

When my brother turned twelve he went to work for old man Canton. The Cantons owned the farm that adjoined our store. The five acres that we owned had once been a part of the Canton place. Fifty years before, one of the Cantons built the store beside the turnpike. Later, he built a three-room house behind the store and several other outbuildings—a chicken house, a cowshed, and a pig pen. An old tobacco barn stood to the west of the store. It had been there for as long as anyone could remember.

My brother finished his homework and left to feed Canton's livestock. Soon I would be working on one of our neighbor's farms. That's how you learned to make a living from the land the way men had always done. I watched as my brother walked away. He carried himself so differently now—his head high, his shoulders back like a soldier. Anyone could see he was rapidly becoming a man. He was tall and strong and well-coordinated, all the things I was not. I would be like him I told myself. But as I watched him duck under the fence and disappear into the pinewoods I thought of old man Canton who was also a man—had been one for many years— a man stooped with pain from his swollen joints, his hands like coarse sandpaper, his nose brown and bulbous as a puff ball. The hawk hung like a kite in the sky above us. Thornton never told me how he felt about being a man.

I would soon find out how I would feel about it. In June I would be twelve. In farm country, a boy became a man at twelve. It was biblical, this passage into manhood. It could not be questioned or discussed. To be a man you had to put away childish things. As a child you did chores. As a man you did work. Chores were not always easy but they were finite—feeding the chickens and gathering the eggs, milking the cow, splitting firewood and bringing it into the wood box. You might not want to do your chores but at least when they were done you were free. Man's work was infinite. Tobacco was the main crop, the cash crop. Men planted, chopped, topped, suckered, cut, cured, stripped, bundled, and sold tobacco. There was corn to be planted, chopped, cut, shucked, shelled and fed to livestock. Hay to be cut, cured, stored, and fed to livestock. Horses, cattle, pigs, chickens, sheep, goats to be bred, birthed, fed, fenced, pastured, shedded, killed and cured, or sold at market. There was not enough time to get to the end of one job before another began. The days lapped into weeks, weeks into months, seasons overlapped. Too much rain. Too little rain. Heat and cold. Thunder and lightning. Flood and drought. Calves born in the swamp after dark. Foxes in the hen house. Bad weather. Bad moons. Bad luck. Bad blood. Bad timing. Bad markets. Bad money. As a man you had to concentrate on the task at hand. Do one job at a time then move to the next. Don't look ahead, don't try to see the future. If you could see to eternity all you would see is work—hard, backbreaking work.

Of course I didn't know this at twelve but it wouldn't have mattered if I had. It was not a choice I was making. I was not asked if I wanted to do it. I was not told I had to do it. It was simply the way things were, the way things always had been for as far back as anyone could remember. I could not say: "I do not want to become a man."

Nineteen-fifty-three might as well have been 1935. The depression was over but the small farms that made up our community of Phoebe had not recovered, and they never would. They survived into the 1950s only because that last generation of family farmers had not yet died off. Their sons, who had fought the war, didn't want to be farmers. And they didn't have to be. There were jobs in cities where the pay was steady and the workday had a beginning and an end. The old men carried on as best they could, but there were too few hands to do the things that had always been done by hand.

Our store stood at the edge of a road that would soon become a major highway, but we didn't cater to the needs of travelers. Our customers were the farm families who lived nearby. Ours was a country store and although we did not have a farm, we were a part of that dying economy.

My brother and I grew up knowing we would one day work on our neighbors' farms. Whether or not our parents thought we would become farmers I don't know. Like the old farmers, they were probably just carrying on a way of life they knew. My brother had been working for the Cantons for two years. He took classes in vocational agriculture at school and was a member of the Future Farmers of America. Two years of doing man's work had changed him. We no longer roamed the woods together. We no longer built forts, dug caves, played at being Indians, went fishing, or did a hundred other things that we had done as children. He had no time for such things. He was now a part of a different world. Even when we had time together he showed little interest in the things of our childhood. Occasionally I felt that even he thought I was a slacker, a daydreamer. He was well on his way to being a man, but in that spring just before I turned twelve, he had a brief relapse.

As children we dreamed of taming a wild animal and roaming the countryside with it as our companion. We knew it was possible to tame wild animals. One of our neighbors was an old man named Crews. My father said he was shell-shocked in the first war. He lived alone in a cabin back in the woods. People said he had all kinds of wild animals living in the cabin with him. We had seen only one of them with our own eyes—a raccoon that perched on Mr. Crews' shoulder when he came to pick up supplies at the store. There was always a sense of excitement when he came walking up the highway with the coon on his shoulder. Even the adults stopped what they were doing and looked. The cars on the highway slowed. Thornton and I were impressed but we were confident we would tame something even more impressive—a mountain lion or a bear.

We were always looking for orphaned animals, but we had little success. We found several baby rabbits and a squirrel but they all died despite our efforts to feed them milk with a medicine dropper. Every year we rescued a few birds, fallen from their nests. We fed them earthworms, dangling them above their open mouths and dropping them. If they lived they returned our kindness by growing wings and flying away.

Then one evening not long after my father's stroke, Thornton brought home a baby skunk he had found in the Canton's barn. He said nothing about it during supper, but afterwards, he took me outside and led me to the place where he had the skunk caged in a peach basket. We were not ignorant of the nature of skunks and the sickening smell they produce, but we knew that Mr. Crews kept several skunks that were as tame as house cats. People said he knew how to "operate" on them when they were young and render them harmless. Our skunk was just a baby. When the time was right we would take it to Mr. Crews for an operation.

Our immediate concern was finding a hiding place, a place where our mother wouldn't find it. We didn't have to ask—we knew she would not approve. There were two small buildings in back of the house but Thornton thought they were too visible from the kitchen window. He didn't want our mother to become suspicious, seeing us going in and out of one of these buildings every day. The only building that was suitable was the old barn. It was on the opposite side and away from the house. The barn was father's garage, where he worked on cars, trucks, tractors —anything mechanical. It was his natural occupation. Opening the store was mother's idea. It appealed to her sense of order and cleanliness. For several years after we moved there he devoted himself to running the store but as the years passed it must have become obvious to him that there was no way to make a living operating a country store. Over mother's objections he started working on cars.

He converted part of the tobacco barn into a garage. He cut an opening through the front wall and poured a concrete slab over part of the dirt floor. With the barn boards he removed to make the opening he made a sliding door that opened and closed to let cars in and out. From the outside it still looked like a barn, its sides covered with weathered vertical boards, unpainted. The roof was metal, with patches of rust. On the side away from the house was a regular door with an old brass padlock. Father never locked the garage. The lock was something left by the previous owner.

Inside the barn was a vast darkness—in my imagination it was a setting for nightmares. It was open from the dirt floor all the way up to the underside of the roof. Tier poles—on which the tobacco was hung for curing—laced the darkness at intervals of four feet vertically and horizontally. At ground level, with the side door open, one could see the shapes of things through a muddy darkness, but up above there was an ancient darkness, a darkness that had been imprisoned when the barn was built, an indelible darkness that even the sharp lines of sunlight that knifed through the cracks could not extinguish. Creatures lived in that darkness. Beetles, spiders, wasps, dirt daubers, lizards. Once a dead bat fell on the hood of a car my father was repairing. But snakes were my worst fear. They wrapped themselves around the tier poles and hung down like lengths of rope, at least that's what happened in the stories the old farmers told. As a child Thornton had shared my fear and we avoided the old building but now as he was becoming a man he scoffed at my fear and insisted on keeping the skunk in the barn. Who could feel comfortable in a building where at any moment snakes might rain down on you.

My father also installed a chain hoist in the old barn. It was attached to a steel beam that rested on two posts about ten feet apart. This mechanical device had a head full of pulleys and wheels through which the chains were wound and guided in such a way that my father, single-handedly, could lift an engine from an automobile. That was the intended use of the hoist. Its other use was at hog killing time when it was used to lift the carcasses of hogs by their hind legs so the blood would drain from their slit throats. Then their bellies were slit and their glistening bowels cascaded down into a washtub.

During that last year before his stroke my father spent more and more time in the old barn— sometimes working late into the night. When my father renovated the barn, he removed the lowest tier of poles to make space to drive a car inside but in the upper part of the barn the poles had been left in place. A long extension cord was looped around one of these poles. A light bulb with a round metal shade over it was attached to the end of the cord. It dangled about eight feet above the floor, dropping a gloomy circle of light on the concrete slab. The hoist lurked just at the edge of the light, the beam and the posts barely visible so that it seemed to hang from the darkness itself. When I looked at it in the dim light it looked like a man hanging from a gallows.

But the garage seemed to suit my father's temperament. Sometimes when I was doing my chores I would hear him whistling. It was something I had never heard him do before. His whistling was more than the scream of air forced through puckered lips. He moved up and down, caught a range of notes and turned them into song. There were slow sad tunes and lively happy ones.

He was twenty years older than my mother and until he met her all he had ever done was tinker with cars. When they married, he bought the store. I imagine he did this to please her, to show her he was settling down to a family life. Storekeeping was in her eyes a cut above farming, but my father liked a challenge—to be given a problem and then

to be left alone to solve it. He found his challenge tinker-
ing with cars. There were plenty of them to repair. Four-
sixty, the road where our store was located, was becoming
a highway. Every family it seemed had a car. Some had two.
The ex-soldiers who had found jobs in town drove into
work every morning. In the evening they drove back to the
country to the ranch-style houses they had built on a lot
cut from the corner of a cornfield on their fathers' farms.
The old farmers were forced to turn more and more to
machines to make up for the lack of help.

Father used to say the only sure thing about a machine
is that sooner or later it will break down. My father did
not *start* an auto repair business. He started by simply helping his customers in the driveway in front of the store. I
suppose it became obvious to him after a while that there
was more demand for engine repair than for the things he
carried in the store. Eventually he made the changes to the
barn and began spending more of his time there.

This was not something that pleased my mother. She
was a farmer's daughter, one of ten children. To her, storekeeping was a respectable occupation. It brought a little
status. And most of all it was orderly and clean. Working
on cars was not. You could not predict when they would
fail or how long it would take to fix them. There were
times when my father didn't come in for supper despite
my mother's calls from the side porch. Once he worked all
night. He didn't like to stop until the job was finished, the
problem solved. In many ways this was sensible, given the
nature of the work, the dirt and grease, the odor of gas and

oil. When he stopped working he had to clean up. There was a shed off the back of our house we called the wash-room. My father would clean himself up there and leave his dirty clothes in the corner for my mother to wash. If he stopped before the job was done, it meant he had to wash up twice. But more than that, I think, once he got into a job nothing else mattered.

My mother's dislike for the old barn was no secret and once my father converted it to a garage she refused to set foot inside the place. My brother, who had no fear of build-ings or anything else scoffed at the idea of snakes falling from the darkness. He decided it was the ideal place to keep the skunk away from mother's critical gaze.

He lifted the padlock and pushed the door open and vanished into the darkness. I waited outside until he found the light and turned it on. The place was littered with parts—engine blocks, transmissions, starters, generators, radiators. I picked my way carefully through them, moving to the open area between the sliding door and the beam where the hoist hung. Thornton searched the perimeter for holes through which the skunk might escape. I waited under the glow of the light bulb until he came back.

"This will do," he said.

He took the basket from me, sat it on the grease-caked floor and removed the lid and I had my first good look at the skunk. It was a beautiful creature, not much bigger than a fist, with a black and white coat that seemed to glow even under the dingy light. It looked up at me with such innocent eyes it was difficult to believe it would someday be able to produce such a disgusting odor.

Thornton had planned well. He had rags, jar tops, water, and some table scraps he had taken from the kitchen. We placed the basket on its side, wedged between an engine block and a toolbox, so the skunk could come and go. We put the rags in the basket to make a bed. Just outside the basket on the floor we arranged the jar tops—one with water, one with food.

The animal showed no interest in our preparations. It would not eat or drink and each time we put it in its bed it immediately got up and walked out on the dirty concrete and stood there looking up at us with eyes that seemed much too big for its body. Finally we gave up. When we left, it did not attempt to follow us. It just stood there staring, until we cut the light out and closed the door.

We visited the skunk after supper every night for the first week. We were a team again, planning adventures with our new companion. We would train it to ride on our shoulders. My brother began calling it Lash LaRue after his favorite cowboy movie star. It was a happy time. I forgot my father's illness and the threat of manhood that hung over me. Even the old barn seemed less frightening than before.

This happiness was short-lived however. The spring planting season arrived and old Canton needed every hour of my brother's time. Thornton often ate supper at the Canton's house and didn't get home till after dark. Saturdays he worked from sun-up till sundown. Sunday was the only day he was free—but we had Sunday school and church and Sunday dinner with relatives. And in the afternoon a steady flow of visitors stopping by to see my father who remained bedridden and silent. After a week, Thornton had no time for our childish adventures. I became the sole keeper of the skunk.

I would like to remember that I was a good keeper. I do remember trying to play with it —holding it in my lap like a cat, talking to it, petting it. But it never warmed to this attention. Its big unblinking eyes were always on me but they revealed nothing other than a general wariness of other creatures. As the days passed it seemed little changed from the first day we put it in the garage. I brought water and food on a regular basis, at least at first, but it had no appetite for what I brought. It did not grow, yet it was not starving. It survived with little physical change there in the darkness of the barn among the rusting car parts and the smell of oil and gas.

My father's stroke dealt a blow to all our lives. A month passed and he was still unable to get out of bed, unable to speak a complete sentence and unable to feed himself. My mother took care of him, ran the store, fixed the meals, kept the house, and washed our clothes. At first she spoke of it as a temporary thing —"until your father gets back on his feet." It was a reasonable expectation. My father was only fifty-six and had always been in good health. Surely he would recover. I remember her saying to someone soon after his stroke: "Maybe it will keep him out of that garage." She seemed cheered at the prospect.

As summer began and the second month of his disability ended, she must have realized that things were not likely to return to normal any time soon. My mother was not unfamiliar with the operation of the store. She worked behind the counter when father was away, though she refused to do so when he was working on cars in the garage. Now it became her full-time job. Once she realized it might remain her job she began to put more and more of her energy into it. She liked people and people liked her. In that respect she was much better suited for the job than my father.

Our house was directly behind the store. It was only a few steps from our door to the back door of the store. During that summer my mother spent a lot of her time hurrying between the two buildings. She continued to open the store at six every morning just as my father had done and kept it open until well after dark, closing time varying with the seasons. Customers trickled in throughout the day and into the evening. Sometimes there would be someone waiting when she opened the door at six, at other times the store might be open an hour or two before the first person came in. It was not a thriving business, selling feed, seed, fertilizer, gas, canned goods, soft drinks, Nabs, and cigarettes—but it kept her busy. She gave me some new chores —washing and drying dishes, hanging clothes on the line—the kind of work she had always done herself. I was still given the freedom to play, to wander about the way my brother and I had always done. However, as that summer approached I found little pleasure in it.

My mother might have continued her Herculean effort indefinitely had it not been for a new complication. After two months in bed, hardly moving and seeming little aware of what was going on around him, my father began falling out of bed. It happened several times in the course of a week, always when he was alone. Each time my mother had to call a neighbor to come over and lift him back into his bed.

It was Saturday in late May, the last Saturday before my birthday and the end of the school year. It was my last day of childhood freedom. I decided to spend it fishing. I dug the worms at the corner of our pigpen. The two young pigs squealed as I dug, hoping I would bring another bucket of slops. Across the way in a distant field, I could see my brother and Mr. Canton and several other men stacking bales of hay on a wagon. It was a fine day, pleasantly warm but not really hot. As I walked behind the garage it occurred to me that I had not fed the skunk for several days.

I was lifting the padlock from the garage door when I heard my mother call. There was an urgency in her voice that startled me. I left the food scraps and the cup of water I was carrying in the grass and ran back behind the garage.

As I came up to the back of the house, she called again. When I rounded the corner she stood in the yard looking down at a bundle of cloth on the ground. At first I thought she had dropped a basket of laundry. Fortunately I didn't smile or say something foolish, for when I got closer I realized that the bundle of clothes was my father. Somehow he had gotten out of bed and made it to the door, opened it and fallen into the yard.

"Where were you?" my mother asked.

"Digging worms."

"Your father has fallen out of bed," she said. That struck me as a curious way of putting it. It was obvious he not fallen from his bed to the yard.

"Is he all right?" I looked down at him. His eyes were closed and he seemed to be peacefully sleeping in the grass.

"Of course he's all right. He just fell . . ." This time she stopped.

An awkward moment followed. I was too old to simply believe what the evidence before me did not support, but too inexperienced to understand why she would not acknowledge my father's strange behavior.

"Where did you think you were going?" my mother said to my father. He was back in his bed again, thanks to a neighbor who happened to stop at the store just as my mother and I struggled to lift him. She ran her hands over his body, feeling his arms, his legs, his ribs, checking for broken bones or blood or bruises, but he had survived the fall without a scratch. She pulled the sheet up over his legs and looked at me.

"Someone has to stay with him," she said. She went to the kitchen and brought back a chair and placed it in the corner of the room.

"Sit!" she said.

I thought this was just another chore my mother was giving me. I would sit there for an hour or two and then I would be free. And in another week I would begin the real work that would make me a man. But it was not an hour or a day or a week my mother had in mind. When the summer ended and the crops were harvested and school was ready to open again, I was still sitting in that room.

Half a century has passed since that long ago summer but even now I have but to close my eyes to feel the slow passing of each hour in that hot and airless room, to see my father's lame eye lurching about, to smell the urine in his bed clothes, to hear the hiss of traffic passing on the hot asphalt outside, and to taste the bitter dust that drifted through the open windows from the fields where my brother was doing a man's work.

My brother grew tall and strong that summer. He became a hard worker who kept his mind on what he was doing. He developed a quiet confidence that the older generation of farmers expected and appreciated in a young man. They told my mother that he was a "natural worker" and she was pleased. I saw very little of him. He was always working. In the evenings when he came in from the fields he helped my mother in the store and by mid-summer he was tending the store alone in the evening so mother could finish her day of work—the washing or cleaning or cooking.

I sat in the same chair, in the same room all day, every day. Often hours passed and I would not see or talk to anyone. Sometimes my mother gave me chores to do, but mostly I did nothing, saw no one, said nothing.

Night crept in like a fog, blurring the familiar objects in the room—the dresser, the chairs, the bed—until my father's face was at last blotted out. Only the window remained, like a movie screen. Outside fireflies blinked in the shadows of the trees. A faint light rippled over the landscape when a car rushed by on the highway and the noise of its passing dimmed for a moment the shrill of crickets and tree frogs.

Sometimes when a customer pulled into the driveway of the store a shaft of light lanced into the dark room illuminating my father's face, his eyes wild and frightened like those of a trapped animal.

They said my brother was a natural worker. Natural work was man's work—hard, repetitive, bone-tiring but at the end of the day, or the end of a season or the end of a life, satisfying. Man's work was predictable. One season followed another. Each brought its share of surprises—storm, drought, flood, fire, and the failure of machines. They were expected and dealt with according to the circumstances. "All in a day's work" was their answer to the unpredictability and the inevitability of a farmer's life.

The failure of the human body also is inevitable and equally unpredictable. We know it will happen—but not to us. Not now, not in the midst of life. We do not expect it to happen—at least, not in one's own family. But when it did happen, the additional work it created fell to the women. The people in our community seldom went to the hospital. Nursing homes were not a part of their vocabulary. The care of the halt and the lame fell to the women. Accidents and epidemics, miscarriage and menopause, illness and old age, lunacy and death lurked at the periphery of woman's work. There was hardly a family around Phoebe without a member whose physical or mental health did not place an additional burden on its wives, mothers, sisters, and daughters.

Who can say what might have become of me had this cup passed from me. Would I be any different today? I knew from a very early age that I did not like farm work or storekeeping or any of the other jobs I saw men doing. It was not the work itself, but the boredom that seemed to hover over it. Even when the men got together socially, as on Sundays when we often gathered at my grandparents' house, my uncles seemed to lack enthusiasm. After the big mid-day meal they sat on the front porch together but conversation was sparse while in the kitchen where I was hiding under a table an excited din of voices competed for attention. The fact that a mountain of dishes was being washed and dried seemed only a byproduct of the real business at hand, gossip. I was too big now to hide in the kitchen and listen to the women gossip. Still, I knew this was not my world.

How does one compare chopping tobacco or getting up hay to sitting hour after hour with an invalid? To the men and the soon-to-be-men, working in the hot summer sun the very idea would have been laughable. Of course, invalids had to be cared for but no fool would think of it as the same as hoeing, suckering, or cutting tobacco. They, the men, were glad to help with the sick and the infirm when a strong hand was needed as when my father struggled out of bed and fell and had to be gotten up. They would stop their work if they were summoned and come on the double.

When my mother thanked them for their trouble, they would say: "Oh, no trouble," as if dealing with the sick was nothing. Or they might say: "Glad to get out of the sun for a few minutes" looking at me, or did I only imagine they were, in my clean shorts and shirt, twelve years old, doing nothing but sitting there drinking a glass of cold lemonade while they worked in the fields.

What did they know of how slowly the time passed in that gloomy, airless room, or of the humiliation of spoon-feeding baby food into your own father's mouth, of lighting his cigarettes and holding them to his lips while he smoked, of learning to shave on someone else's face. What did they know of the groans, the coughing fits, the showers of spit, the snot rags, bedpans, enemas, rubber sheets? Had they ever been locked in a hot room and forced to listen to the tortured sleep of a man whose nightmares perhaps provided the only relief from his terrible consciousness?

Was I born with a "lazy streak" as they sometimes said? Was it true that my real talent was for getting out of work? Was I "half-asleep-half-the time?" Couldn't keep my mind on what I was doing? A dreamer? Was I a little "slow?" Were these things people really said or did I only imagine them?

A chain hoist does not look like a man. It's not made to lift a man. A hoist is a clever device designed so a man can lift a three hundred pound engine out of a car. But it was a man's face I saw up there in the gloom of my father's garage. A familiar face, though not recognizable, a grotesque fig-ure with a hooked nose and arms—arms as long and limp as chains, rattling and rising disjointedly like the arms of a marionette. The pulleys whirled as the chains sprang to life. I was being lifted. I felt a movement beneath my feet as if the earth itself were being hoisted up into a dark hell. I looked down—the hooked-nosed man has bound my feet. I am strung up like a hog. I am upside down, swinging and twisting. Beneath me, looking up, is a sea of faces. Something drips from my nose . . . warm . . . warm and dark. Drip . . . drip . . . drip . . . drip. Then it begins to run, to trickle, to gush . . .

I open my eyes and see a ripple of light flicker in the room. A car is passing on the highway. Across the room my brother is snoring softly. I am still in a half-dream state, searching the faces for the hooked-nose man, still feeling the gush from my nose. I put my hand to my nose expecting to feel blood but as I drift up out of sleep the gush of blood turned into the unmistakable, repulsive odor of skunk.

The smell of a skunk was not all that unusual. There were lots of them living in the forest and fields around us. On the highway they were sometimes struck by passing cars and fought back with the only weapon they had. Occasionally they scored a direct hit and the car carried the odor along the highway for miles.

I finally went back to sleep. When I got up that morning the odor was still in the air. My brother had already left for another day of work in the fields. When I came into the kitchen my mother was washing Mason jars at the sink. A bushel basket of half runners, freshly picked, sat on the floor. It would be my morning's work to string and snap the beans while I sat watching my father. In the afternoon my mother would can them, working around the customers who came by the store.

"Smells like we had a visitor last night," she said. She sat the last canning jar on the drain board and went to check on my father. I poured a bowl of corn flakes, put milk and sugar on them—but after a couple of spoonfuls, I wasn't hungry anymore.

"He's still asleep," she said when she came back. "You'll have to feed him when he wakes up. It smells even stronger in the bedroom. I hope we don't have a skunk living under the house. When I was a girl we had a family of them living under our house. Something frightened them one night and the house smelled for a week. We had to eat out of doors to get away from it. It made you sick at your stomach just to think of food with that smell in the air. Oh, it was a lot stronger than this. This is nothing but a baby skunk smell."

A baby skunk smell? The phrase startled me. Was my mother saying that baby skunks were able to produce the scent, or was she merely making a size comparison between the two smells?

Sometime earlier in the summer, my brother told me to take the skunk out in the woods and set it free. I hadn't done so, not because I had any great love for the animal, but I had come to depend on it to keep my courage up when I went to the garage.

The old building was like a haunted house, it frightened and it fascinated me. Having the skunk there meant that I had to go there.

As soon as I finished breakfast my mother got me started on the beans. She liked things done her way. Each time she gave me a new chore she insisted on "getting me started." I took the beans back to the bedroom where my father was still sleeping. My mother followed with a clean pot and an old bucket and some newspapers.

I sat the bushel of beans down on the floor as instructed and sat down in the chair. The beans went to my left where I could reach them, the pot to my right, the bucket in front of me. She folded the paper and placed it in my lap so it formed a well between my legs. She told me to fill the well with beans. She took a long green bean and snapped the ends off, peeling with them the thin strings along the spine of the pod. Then she broke the bean into three pieces and dropped them into the empty pot. The strings she dropped in the old bucket at my feet. This was her way, except that I was to drop the strings back onto the newspaper and dump them in the bucket only after finishing all the beans I had put in the well. I had been stringing beans for her since I was four or five years old, but each time she had to get me started. It was not that she considered me a slow learner. She was merely afraid that if she didn't get me started, I would be tempted to try a different arrangement—I might reverse the basket and the pot for instance—to find a new way of stringing beans. Of course this would be a foolish waste of time since her way was obviously the best way.

Just as she finished her demonstration we heard a customer pulling into the driveway in front of the store. She left and I began processing the beans from left to right.

The skunk smell in the bedroom was indeed stronger than in the rest of the house. I remained uneasy. I tried to remember the last time I had taken food and water to the garage. It had been a few days, maybe even a week. The trouble was, the skunk never seemed to eat anything I fed it. Scraps of moldy food piled up. It seemed useless to keep on bringing food. It was clearly time to get rid of it. I hoped I hadn't waited too long already.

I thought I felt someone looking at me but when I looked my father's eyes were closed. I was stringing beans as fast as I could but the bottom of the big pot wasn't even covered. I thought I might have a chance to slip out to the garage after I finished the first lap-full if my father didn't wake up.

After my father's stroke my mother slept in the day bed on the far side of the room. During the day it served as a sofa for the visitors who came to see my father. He seldom tried to speak, and when he did it was almost impossible to understand him. There were lots of visitors. On Sunday, the room would sometimes be full of relatives and neigh-bors. Most of them stood in the corners of the room and talked to each other around my father's bed. The oldest ones or the ones in ill health sat on the day bed or in the chair where I sat all week.

Each visit followed the same pattern. The visitor entered the room and immediately went over to the bed and spoke to my father. Sometimes he would look at them with his good eye while his other eye rolled beneath its drooped lid. At first they would look directly at him as they talked but under his unblinking gaze they soon dropped their eyes and stared at his hands that my mother had folded on top of the bed cover. Their one-sided conversations would go on for as long as the visitor could think of something to say. Then the visitor would pause, look up again into my father's eyes and smile, pat him on the legs, and drift away. My father's gaze never left them until they turned away, but the eye never gave any indication that communication had taken place. I do not know why but it was my impression that my father hated these visits, hated people standing over him, around him, filling up his space.

I looked at him again lying there on his back, his eyes closed. And I knew he wasn't sleeping. He was hiding deep inside himself. It is a trick I have learned over the years. It's a clever way to escape confrontation but ultimately it can be self-destructive. Of course my father knew the trick before his stroke, but afterwards, lying there day after day, he perfected it to the point that the light beam of his consciousness was compressed by great force of will to a pure hard diamond.

When I finished the first lap-full of beans, I lifted the newspaper and dumped the strings into the bucket. I laid the paper aside and stood up. With the basket, the pot and the bucket surrounding me I had to move my feet carefully to free myself. I did not want to move anything for fear my mother would find her arrangement disordered.

Standing up I suddenly got a stronger whiff of the skunk odor and I knew I had to get out to the garage as soon as possible. I walked over and stood by my father. His eyelids remained closed but I could see the movement of his crippled eye beneath the lid.

"You want some breakfast?" I asked. I was testing. I knew there would be no answer.

The room was silent. The eye continued to move but the lids remained closed. The silence was broken by the sound of a drink delivery truck pulling into the driveway of the store—an abrupt clatter of bottles as the rear wheels dropped from the edge of the pavement. The delivery would keep my mother busy in the store so I wouldn't have to worry about her returning to the bedroom anytime soon.

It was my father I was concerned about. I would like to believe I was a diligent, concerned caregiver during those times I was forced to sit all day in my father's room. I was not. I took every opportunity to deceive my mother and escape from my station. Over the long weeks of that summer I had studied her daily routine so that I knew when she was likely to check in on my father and me. During those times I was always in my chair. But the other times when I did not expect her to be there I often slipped out into the backyard and wandered about, daydreaming and doing nothing. It was during my absences that my father attempted his own escapes and would end up helpless on the floor. Each time this happened I had to explain to my mother why I had not stopped him from getting up, why I had not called her sooner. After all, this was my responsibility—to keep him from getting out of bed.

Had he continued to make these escapes I would have had no choice but to stay with him every minute, but after a couple of close calls, he stopped trying to go wherever it was he wanted to go and I was free to slip out without fear of coming back and finding him on the floor.

I often felt he was telling me to leave. He did this by closing his eyes and feigning sleep, just as he was doing now. I would like to believe he was sympathetic to my boredom and was kindly giving me his permission to go out and play. But that was not the feeling I got. He had his own reasons for wanting me out of there. They were reasons I was not old enough to understand.

Although my father had not spoken a complete sentence since the stroke he and I had our own form of communication. Others talked to him as if there was no intelligence behind the glazed eyes and the vacant expression on his face. They tended to shout as if they thought a loud voice necessary. If I spoke at all I spoke quietly. His eyes responded, or more specifically, his good eye responded. Usually I did not have to say anything. When he looked at me I knew what he wanted. His requests were simple. He wanted food or drink. He needed to urinate or defecate. He was too hot or too cold. And most often, he wanted to smoke. When his eyes were open but he was not looking at me he wanted nothing. When his eyes were closed, he was usually sleeping. But increasingly I was becoming aware of this new message coming from his closed eyes. I knew it meant he wanted me to leave.

I looked back at the basket of green beans. I knew I did not have long. I did not want to fall behind on stringing the beans or my mother would become suspicious. I wished I could simply return to my chair and not go outside but the smell of skunk and the will of my father combined to drive me from the room.

My parents' bedroom had its own door to the outside. It opened onto the yard on the east side of the house. From there I slipped around the corner of the bedroom and I was safely hidden behind the house. It was already hot in the sunshine and the air was hazy with heat. I looked out over the fields. Someone was driving down the lane to the Canton house. A cyclone of dust rose above the hedgerow. I was sure it was my brother. He didn't have a license but Canton let him drive his old pickup on the farm and sometimes even on the highway.

Outside there was only a faint odor of skunk. As I approached the garage I noticed that the padlock was not hooked in the hasp the way we always left it. It was never locked but we hooked it in the latch to keep the door from blowing open. The door was slightly ajar and the lock lay on the ground. I wondered if my brother had come out earlier. Perhaps he had intentionally left the door open so the skunk could escape. But why was the lock on the ground? Had he been frightened by a sudden appearance of the skunk, its tail curled back aiming a blast at him?

I found a long stick and, standing to the side of the door, I used it to gently push the door open. I stared into the dark interior for a long time but I could only see the thin lines of sunlight falling through the cracks. Finally I stepped quietly inside and stood very still letting my eyes adjust to the darkness. Inside the odor was very strong and my empty stomach began to churn.

I could make out the litter of car parts on benches and shelves, hanging from nails on the walls. On the oil-caked floor lay a pair of pliers and a ball peen hammer just the way my father had left them. I moved cautiously toward the basket. I could see several jar tops with rotting food in them and one that was dry. Maybe the skunk had died of thirst. I looked back at the door. Perhaps the skunk had escaped. After all someone had left the door ajar. Perhaps it was back in the woods with its own kind, happy and free.

But something was moving through the strips of sun-light. It was Lash LaRue. "Lash," I whispered as the skunk came out from behind a radiator. The time was slipping away. My mother might come back to the bedroom at any moment.

Catching the skunk was no problem. It never resisted being touched or petted though it never returned the affec-tion. But picking it up and carrying it out into the bright sunlight was risky. The shock of the sunlight and the fear it might feel being taken from its home could trigger a spray.

I knelt beside it. Its gaze never left me. It seemed to sense that something bad was going to happen. As I curled my fingers under its belly and picked it up, it stiffened, and its tail curled slightly. I tried to point it away from me but it twisted itself with a surprising strength so that my face became the target.

I hurried toward the door and without thinking I passed directly beneath the chain hoist. Something touched my hair, then dropped down on me and slid across my neck and shoulder, its body slick and cool as silk. I seemed to leave my body for a moment and be lifted up into the dark purgatory above myself. From there I looked down and saw myself frozen beneath the dangling ends of the chains, my hands gripping the animal I held too tightly, its body tensed again, its tail curled like a clock spring. And I felt a rope of ice scalding my cheek, my nose, my chest—the dark shiny coil dangling from the hook on the lift chain.

My father's taste in clothes was practical. As a store-keeper he wore sturdy cotton shirts and pants. My mother washed and starched and ironed them. Sharp creases gave shape to the sleeves and pants legs. For church, weddings and funerals he owned two suits. One was called the "new suit" to distinguish it from the other which I presume was older. Neither was new but one was a darker color than the other. His church shirts, if he had more than one, were all white. His shoes were black. His only extravagance was a red and black silk necktie, *Made in France*. How he came to pos-sess this exotic article of clothing I do not know. He wore it infrequently. It was not a "Sunday tie" and there were few social events in Phoebe where it would have been appropri-ate. I have a vague memory of him wearing it to a Christmas party in Lynchburg hosted by the wholesale company that supplied most of the stock for the store, and of my mother's disparaging comments. The tie had no recognizable fea-tures. It was a statement in color. A bold statement, what I would call today romantic. With his dark hair combed back and his dark skin and eyes, he looked Mediterranean, like a movie star or a gangster. Sometimes in my memory I see a little twist of a smile forming on his lips.

Had it been a snake hanging down from the hook of the hoist brushing my cheek with its cold skin, I might remember it with a laugh as just another time I was frightened as a child. After all, I had always suspected snakes to be hanging from the tier poles. But it was not a snake. It was my father's necktie.

I trembled at the edge of understanding that terrible moment long ago when I discovered my father's necktie fashioned into a hangman's noose dangling from the hook of the chain hoist. It is impossible for me to say how much I understood then, to separate that knowing from what I have learned and come to believe over the years. I can only tell you what I recall doing after I made the discovery.

I maintained my hold on the skunk, and though its tail remained cocked, it did not spray me. I took it outside and released it into the dry stream bed that was the back border of our land. When I put it down it sat there without moving, looking up at me with pleading eyes. I turned and ran from it, ran back to the garage where I untied the silk tie from the hook and slipped the noose loop through its knot and the silk released its wrinkles and became a necktie again. I folded it and put it in my pocket.

I did not linger. I knew the skunk would try to find its way back into the garage again. It was the only home it knew. I stepped out into the sunlight again and pulled the door closed behind me and fixed the latch. I bent down and picked up the old padlock and hooked it in the hasp.

With both hands I squeezed the lock shut until I heard the locking pin snap into place.

I went back to my father's room. My mother was still busy in the store. My father was pretending to sleep but I could sense he knew I was there. I did not hesitate for fear I would lose my nerve. I gripped the sheet and the bed-spread that were covering him and peeled them back all the way to the foot of the bed. The odor trapped beneath them rose like fumes from hell. His lids popped open and his good eye skewered me.

His bedclothes and his bedding had to be changed frequently due to his "accidents," as my mother called them. She had become expert at changing the bed with him in it. With my help she would move him to one side of the bed, then unmake the other side and remake it with clean sheets. She would undress and wash him, redress him, and with my help move him to the clean side. When the job was completed, we would move him back to the center and she would tuck the sheets in. She could do all this quickly and neatly. I could not. But the bed had to be stripped, my father had to be stripped. I had already decided my mother should never know what happened.

My father was a small man. Lying there on the white sheet, his left side shriveled from the stroke, he seemed even smaller. I wondered if I could pick him up. In a few years I would grow to be a much bigger man than my father, but on that August morning I had only a child's strength.

I reached down to push him toward the side of the bed. I avoided looking into his eyes, fearing what I might see there. As my hands touched his side his right hand came up and stopped me. I looked up. The defiance was gone now and what I saw was a look of resignation, something I had never seen in my father before. It only lasted a moment and then he mumbled a word.

"Wait!"

He raised his right leg and swung it to the side of the bed. Then, hooking his knee over the edge he pulled himself across the bed. He reached back with his right hand and grasping the headboard began pulling himself into a sitting position. I stared at him in amazement. I won't say that it was easy. It was not. It was a struggle—but a practiced struggle—and in the end he was standing on his own with his hand against the wall for balance.

I stripped the covers from the bed, balled them into a tight ball, and put them by the outside door. I left the rubber sheet in place covering the mattress and remade the bed with clean sheets. I could not look at my father and in my mind he became someone else—someone I didn't know but was bound to help in this unfortunate situation. He was struggling without success to get out of his pajamas. The smell was strongest on his legs. I unbuttoned his pajama top. Unlike his face and arms, the skin on his chest and stomach was white. The curly black hair lay like a tangle of fish hooks on his chest. I offered my hand to steady him as I shucked the sleeve over his right arm down to the hand that was holding the wall, but he ignored it.

By force of will he took his hand from the wall, teetered a bit, then balanced himself on his right leg while I slipped the sleeve over his hand. The hand then moved quickly back to the wall. I bent down holding my breath against the smell and worked the pajama bottoms down his legs. He lifted one foot. I slipped the pajamas under it. Then, very slowly his other foot arched just enough for me to pull the garment free. When he was completely naked I did not look at him —only parts of him—his feet, his knees—his withered hand hanging by his white thigh. I got soap and water in a pan and washed his knees and legs. By now the smell had dissipated and hung in the room like a smell of mold or wet wool. I dried him with a towel and rubbed his legs with alcohol. I even got some of my mother's hand lotion that smelled like roses and put it on him.

As I drew my hand away from his knee a drop of water splattered on my knuckles and I heard him heave for breath. When I looked up I saw the quivering chin, the wet nostrils, the steady ribbon of tears sliding down to the point of his chin, collecting, quivering, then falling.

It all turned out quite well. I got my father back to bed and took the clothing outside, hid it and later washed it until the smell was gone. A few days later I found the skunk dead in the highway. There was no odor, just a small mat of black and white fur flattened against the pavement. My father lived another six years. He even learned to walk and to talk again after a fashion. And by the following summer I was free to work in the fields, but I did it only to earn a little money. I knew by then it would not make me a man. That even if it would, I did not want to be one. I kept my father's necktie for many years—first, hidden in my secret place in the wall of my closet along with other treasures; a broken arrowhead I'd found, a pinup of Ava Gardner, an Indian head penny, and the first love letters I ever received. In high school I dreamed of being invited to a sophisticated party somewhere, in some exotic place, where I would appear wearing my father's necktie and be admired and envied by all in attendance. Such a party was never given, or if it was, I was not invited.

Later, when I left home I carried these things with me locked in a small wooden box. I was in the Army. I worked. I went to school. In 1968 in the City where I was living in a loft with a dozen other people, I knew the party had begun at last. I took the tie from my treasure box and put it on with my faded work shirt and jeans. I tied it first with a simple knot. I was pleased when I looked in the mirror. The tie was unique, just as I remembered it. But something was not right. I loosened the knot and tried to affect a more casual look. This was 1968. Casual. Formal. Those terms were obsolete. Your style had to be far out, outrageous. I looked at myself again and again and finally it came to me. I removed the tie and fashioned it into a hangman's noose, slipped it over my head so that the knot stood up behind my left ear. The wide field of sensuous colors stuck out of the knot like a tongue and curled behind me. Everyone loved it. I walked the streets to rave reviews. Friends and strangers wanted to "hang" with me. For a brief moment

I was The Man. But quickly my fame faded. I continued wearing the tie—it seemed to become a part of me—but I gave up the noose.

That could have been the end of the story, but then I fell in love. The tie's importance in my life faded. I still wore it from time to time but it was just another rag, a part of my wardrobe of rags.

It was a fine spring day in 1970 when my love and I bought a kite at a shop on Christopher Street. We walked to the park and assembled its parts. It was a great dragon affair, a kite to brag on, to explore the clouds, but when we let it go in the breeze it bucked and twisted like a wild stallion. Several times we nearly lost it as it spiraled downward out of our control, but at the last instant it swooped up again, just inches from the waves. Finally we coaxed it within reach and brought it down. I knew what was needed. My brother and I had flown kites together all the years of our childhood. It needed a tail.

The silk slipped easily from the collar of my shirt and there I was tying my father's necktie to the tail of our kite. This time the dragon not only twisted and bucked and spiraled, it ascended into the heavens, with a head of steam so great the spinning spool burned my fingers.

Three clouds like puffs from a steam whistle dotted the sky. As it passed in front of one of them I got a last look at the long bright tail of the dragon. I did not know how much cord we had on the spool. I let it run on and on until the tension on the line snapped and I was left with an empty spool.

Proceedings

PLACE: Mosley County Courthouse, Phoebe, Virginia
TIME: 7th Day of June, 1954

These were some who were present that day:

Eliot Wise, who was janitor at the Phoebe School. He had not seen the accidents but had come along shortly after they had happened. He was fond of telling people that he had been the first on the scene, that he had maintained from the beginning that there was something strange about the Moore boys' running away, that he had always thought that the Kinds boy was a queer bird, that he had known all four boys real well, that he had heard that Franklin Moore had sent his boys off with their mother to Tennessee so they couldn't be called on to testify, that he had told Judge Hicks from the beginning that he ought to take a good look into the matter, that the police hadn't done more than a halfway job, that one policeman he knew of had been out chasing after the pigs the minute he arrived on the scene, and that the real problem had started at the school where kids were doing pretty much what they pleased these days.

What he didn't tell people was that he too had chased pigs all over Franklin Moore's place that day and that the cut-up carcass of one of them was now curing in his smokehouse.

William Pumphrey, the state policeman who had been cruising the highway several miles from Franklin Moore's farm when he got the call from the dispatcher concerning the accidents. A week later, he filed a report at state police headquarters without even having gotten to talk with the only eyewitnesses of the incident, Gerald and Aubrey Moore. He had been by the Moore place on several occasions looking for them. The first time, Edna Moore had told him that the boys were too upset to talk about the accidents. When he returned two days later, he was told by Franklin that they had gone with their mother to Tennessee "for a rest." His report concluded that there were many questions that would have to be answered before the incident could be judged entirely accidental. One of these questions was: What had happened that made the Kinds boy run out in the road with no pants on?

Samuel Lange, the Phoebe County sheriff, whose report of the accidents read much the same as William Pumphrey's, because most of it had been taken directly from Pumphrey's report. He had spent much of the evening and night of the accidents rounding up pigs. As he told people later: "Those bastards would have caused another half-dozen wrecks if I hadn't got some men together and caught them."

Vernon Delaney, whose farm adjoined Franklin Moore's. He had been working in the fields when he heard the commotion and had looked up just in time to see the tractor-trailer flip over on its side. Months before some-one had shot one of his beagles. He had told his wife then that some hunter must have mistaken it for a rabbit, but in his heart he believed the Miles boy had done it, and done it on purpose.

Alice Delaney, Vernon's wife, who was afraid of the whole Miles family and wondered why Franklin Moore had ever taken them on as tenants on his farm.

Blanche Bingham, second grade school teacher at Phoebe School and old maid sister of Alice Delaney, who had seen the four boys playing by the road and would normally have stopped and told them to go on home had it not been for the half gallon of ice cream she'd bought after school. It was melting in the seat beside her because she'd lingered for twenty minutes in the drugstore trying to pick out a laxative that would do her some good.

Willie Ray Goodwin, who worked in the drugstore and who sold Miss Blanche Bingham a package of Black Draught on the day of the accidents.

Edward Moore, who had always thought his brother, Frank-lin, had two of the best tenant families in the county working his farm. He had heard that the Kindses were a weird lot and that old man Miles drank too much, but they were hard workers. He knew it was true that both families had left the county, although he did not know if the rumors that Frank-lin had ordered them to leave were true or not. He hadn't known either the Miles or the Kinds boy except by sight, but he knew that both of them had worked out in the fields like men ever since they had been on Franklin's place. That was more than he could say for Franklin's own boys. It was generally agreed that they took after their mother.

Vera Moore, Edward's wife, who was childless and who had gossiped relentlessly about her nephews, Gerald and Aubrey, since the day of the accidents.

Edna Moore, Franklin's wife, who was not originally from Phoebe and who some people thought of as uppity, especially in the way she dressed her children. It was often said among the women that she needed a girl in the family so she'd "loose her grip on the boys."

Franklin Moore, who owned three hundred of the best acres of farm land in the county, who had twice been elected to the County Board of Supervisors, and who was not afraid to let his oldest boy, Gerald, take the witness stand and tell what he knew of the accidents. He was only ashamed of the way his wife had dressed the boys. She didn't understand the way people were in Phoebe and he had never found a way of getting it across to her.

Wayne Link, who ran the Purina Feed Store in Phoebe and who had been off at a Purina Sales meeting on the day of the accidents.

Ann Link, Wayne's wife, who had gone to the Kinds' house once collecting for the Cancer Crusade and had been told that "the Lord would cure those who needed curing."

Reverend David Daniel, minister of the Mt. Hope Baptist Church, who had buried the Miles boy. So far as he knew that was the only time any of that family had been inside a church.

Virgil Reese, a retarded "boy" of thirty-four who attended all court sessions, public meetings, and church services, and who went largely unnoticed wherever he was.

William Cain, Virgil Reese's stepfather, who did odd jobs—primarily hauling trash and garbage—for the people of Phoebe. He wife was a distant kin of the Kindses but he'd never had much to do with them.

Billy Ray Cain, William's natural son, who sold bootleg whiskey, frequently to Walter Miles, and on one occasion to the boy, Raymond Miles.

Len Cain, Billy Ray's brother, who had caught three of the pigs and sold them to a farmer in the next county.

James Metcalfe, who published the county's only newspaper and who had done much to stir up the curiosity of all those present, including the seventy-four other men and women not named above who filled the courtroom to capacity.

These were some who were not present:

Joseph Papsco, the Pennsylvania truck driver whose rig had been involved in the accidents. He had told the police, and anyone else who cared to listen, all he knew about the accidents: "There was something damn queer going on. That boy was out in the road with his pants down around his ankles. I never saw him till the last minute. And then those other two, I saw them after I crawled out of the cab, standing up there holding hands like a couple of girls. They never even came up to see what happened. When I was a boy, I'd of run a mile to see a good wreck."

Walter Miles and his wife, Marian, who had been summoned by the court.

John Kinds and his wife, Beatrice, also summoned by the court.

Alice Daniel, the wife of Reverend David Daniel, who believed in her heart that idle curiosity and gossip were the works of the devil.

Aaron Hicks, Mosley County Judge, whose decision it had been to order the inquiry. He had asked the solicitor to summon fourteen people, although he had no intention of calling anyone but Franklin Moore's oldest boy, Gerald, to the stand. He had heard the rumor that Franklin had sent the boys to their mother's home in Tennessee, but he had called Franklin and gotten his assurance that the boys would be present for the inquiry. Having been a judge for eighteen years, he did not believe any of the rumors he had heard, but he felt that it was important that the Moore boys' side of the story be told publicly, so he had taken the unusual step of calling for a public judicial inquiry. He wanted the truth to be known and he felt that the courtroom would call forth that truth. He had hoped that the truth would not lend credence to the gossip.

Melvin Russell, court solicitor.

Evelyn Hicks, Judge Aaron Hicks' daughter-in-law and clerk of the court.

Proceedings:

Clerk: Oyez. Oyez. Oyez. All rise for the Judge. Be seated.

Judge: Would the Clerk please read the notice of inquest.

Clerk: By order of Judge Aaron D. Hicks, a public judicial inquest will be convened on June 7, 1954 at the Mosley County Courthouse at 2 p.m. to hear all evidence regarding the tragic and unusual accident that occurred on May 2nd

1954 on U.S. Route 460, approximately two miles west of the town of Phoebe.

Judge: I have ordered this inquest so that we can bring together the facts concerning this unfortunate matter. I want to make it clear that this is in no way a criticism of the reports filed by the sheriff's office and the state police. However, these very reports point out that there are many questions as yet unanswered. And there is so much rumor and misinformation being passed about as truth . . . I have summoned a number of you here today to testify as to what you saw, or what you know, or have heard. But I believe it is of utmost importance that we hear first the testimony of one of those who was an eye witness to the events of that afternoon. Please call Gerald Moore.

Clerk: Gerald Arlington Moore, please come forward. State your full name for the court.

Gerald: Gerald Moore . . . Gerald Arlington Moore.

Clerk: Raise your right hand. Do you swear to tell the truth, the whole truth and nothing but the truth so help you God?

Gerald: Yes, sir . . . Yes, I do.

Judge: Gerald, were you present when the accident of May 2nd occurred?

Gerald: Yes, sir.

Judge: Did you actually see the accident?

Gerald: Yes . . . Your Honor.

Judge: Tell us in your own words the events leading up to the accident, everything that happened after you got off the school bus that afternoon, or anything that happened that day—or on other days—that might be . . . that might have a bearing on what happened that afternoon. Do you understand, Gerald?

Gerald: Yes, sir.

Judge: Go ahead then.

Gerald: Well, we got off the bus same as always.

Judge: Who got off the bus?

Gerald: Ray, Emmitt, Aubrey, and me.

Judge: That would be Raymond Miles, Emmitt Kinds, and your brother, Aubrey Moore?

Gerald: Yes, sir.

Judge: For the benefit of the court, you must be very specific.

Gerald: Yes, sir.

Judge: Now then, you and Emmitt Kinds and Raymond Miles were all in the eighth grade together, were you not?

Gerald: Yes, sir.

Judge: And your brother, Aubrey, is in the second?

Gerald: Yes, sir.

Judge: Go on with your story, Gerald.

Gerald: We got off the bus at the road that goes up to our house. Ray and Emmitt . . . Raymond Miles and Emmitt Kinds live . . . well, they used to live, further along the road, down below our house.

Judge: Raymond and Emmitt's fathers were tenants on your father's farm at that time, were they not?

Gerald: Yes, sir.

Judge: Continue.

Gerald: After the bus pulled off, we stood around by the side of the highway.

Judge: Why did you stay there, Gerald?

Gerald: Ray wanted to, so we stayed with him. He was throwing rocks at a can in the ditch. He liked fooling around on the highway.

Judge: Did Emmitt Kinds usually stay with the rest of you when you were playing beside the highway?

Gerald: No, sir.

Judge: Why did he stay with you on this particular day?

Gerald: I don't know.

Judge: There must have been some reason, if he'd never stayed before. I know for a fact he wasn't the kind of boy that stood around on the highway throwing rocks at a can.

Gerald: I guess . . . I guess he didn't want Ray throwing rocks at him anymore.

Judge: Raymond threw rocks at Emmitt?

Gerald: Sometimes he did. Emmitt usually walked off ahead of us after we got off the bus and Ray would pick up gravel from the edge of the highway and throw it at Emmitt as we walked down the road. They never hurt Emmitt . . . they were just pieces of gravel.

Judge: Why did Raymond throw gravel at Emmitt? Was he mad at him for some reason?

Gerald: No, sir. Ray just never liked Emmitt. He said the Kindses were Holy Rollers and that everybody knew Holy Rollers were crazy. He said Emmitt was a sissy . . . he was always telling Emmitt he was a sissy. He pushed him in the girl's bathroom one time. He said that's where Emmitt ought to have to go to pee.

Judge: What did you think of Emmitt, Gerald? Did you think he was a sissy?

Gerald: He was kind of a sissy. He wasn't like the other boys at school.

Judge: Tell us about that. What was different about him?

Gerald: He talked in a kind of whisper but you could hear him real plain if you listened. But sometimes, even though I heard him I didn't know what he was talking about. He mostly just stayed to himself. At recess he usually stayed in the room and read the Bible. Somebody said they saw him praying once when he was in the room by himself. If he came outside he never played with the boys. He walked around by himself until it was time to go in. Or sometimes he would talk to the girls.

Judge: Gerald, did Emmitt Kinds like girls?

Gerald: Yes, sir, I guess he did.

Judge: And Raymond Miles, did he like girls?

Gerald: Oh, yes, sir, he was crazy about them, but he never would've talked to them. Not like Emmitt did.

Judge: Is there anything else, Gerald, that Emmitt did or said that made you think he was different from other boys?

Gerald: Sometimes . . . sometimes he talked about . . . about sin.

Judge: What did he say about sin?

Gerald: He told Ray it was a sin for him to kill crows even when they were eating the corn right out of your fields. He said sin beget sin and that someday somebody might treat Ray the same way he was treating those crows.

Judge: Was this a threat? Did Emmitt mean he might someday harm Raymond?

Gerald: No, it wasn't a threat. Emmitt would never have tried anything with Ray. Ray was tough . . . he'd flunked two grades in school already. He was ten times stronger than Emmitt.

Judge: He was speaking only from a religious point of view?

Gerald: I guess so. It was usually religion things he was talking about when you couldn't understand what he meant. He told Ray that sin was a boomerang . . . no matter how hard you threw it, it always came right back at you.

Judge: And he thought Raymond was sinning by killing crows?

Gerald: Yes, sir, he said it was wrong to kill anything. He said since God made everything, then one thing had as much right to live as another. But Ray told him that as long as he had a gun and the crow was eating his corn, the crow didn't have any rights . . . unless the crow had a gun and was a better shot than him. Emmitt said that on the day of judgment the crow wouldn't need a gun . . . it would be armed with God's righteousness. He said the Lord's wrath was mightier than a cannon . . . someday, he said, we would all face that wrath . . . someday, he said, we were all going to die. Ray told him he wasn't afraid of dying. "I fell off a barn once," Ray told him, "and near got killed. I broke three ribs and it hurt pretty bad too . . . so don't tell me about dying." But Emmitt said it wasn't the hurting that was bad about dying, it was knowing you were all alone. He told us about his grandmother dying— how they were all standing around in her room but she kept saying "I just wish somebody would come with me." Different ones of the family kept going up to her and saying: "We're all here, gran'mama, right here with you." But she didn't seem to hear them. So they sent Emmitt over to stand by her bed and she said: "I wish somebody would hold my hand." So they made Emmitt take hold of her hand. Finally she opened her eyes and said: "Emmitt, is that you?" And when he said yes, she said, "I wish you could be here with me." He squeezed her hand and told her he was right there, but she just closed her eyes again and said: "I just wish somebody would come by and stay with me this last little while."

Judge: What did Raymond say to that?

Gerald: Nothing. But it was that day, after school when he first started throwing rocks at Emmitt.

Judge: How long ago was that?

Gerald: Last fall, when we first started eighth grade.

Judge: So Raymond threw rocks at Emmitt for the whole school year?

Gerald: Not every day . . . just whenever he felt like it.

Judge: What did you do when Raymond threw rocks at Emmitt . . . did you ever ask him to stop?

Gerald: No, sir.

Judge: Did you ever throw rocks at Emmitt?

Gerald: Some . . . sometimes I did.

Judge: And why did you throw rocks at him?

Gerald: Ray . . . Ray made us . . .

Judge: By us, do you mean Aubrey also threw rocks at Emmitt?

Gerald: Sometimes.

Judge: And Raymond Miles made you do it?

Gerald: Yes, sir.

Judge: How did he make you?

Gerald: He said if we didn't . . . didn't do it, he'd kill us. He said he'd shoot us with his father's rifle. He said he'd claim it was an accident.

Judge: Did you really believe he'd do that?

Gerald: I didn't think he would . . . but I saw him shoot a cat once for no reason at all.

Judge: Did you tell your father about this threat?

Gerald: Aubrey did.

Judge: And did he talk to Raymond?

Gerald: No, sir . . . he talked to us. He said we were big enough to take care of ourselves. He said nobody was going to shoot anybody on his place.

Judge: But you were still afraid of Raymond?

Gerald: No, sir, I wasn't afraid . . . but he was bigger than me. He'd already flunked two grades.

Judge: Did he ever actually do anything to you?

Gerald: He hit Aubrey in the back of the head with a rock once.

Judge: Was this when he was trying to force the two of you to throw rocks at Emmitt?

Gerald: No, sir, this was after he told Aubrey he was going to take his pants off and Aubrey ran from him. He was always saying he was gonna take somebody's pants off.

He thought it was funny . . . making someone walk around with no pants on.

Judge: Did he ever actually take anyone's pants off?

Gerald: Only Emmitt's . . .he tried to take his off that day after we got off the bus. That's the only time he ever did it . . . but he was always talking about it. He was always making fun of our clothes. He thought it was sissy to wear clean clothes . . . his clothes were always dirty and his pants were too big . . . he had to pleat them around his waist with his belt to keep them up. The belt was too big too but he punched extra holes in it to make it fit.

Judge: Was he ashamed of his clothes, Gerald?

Gerald: Oh, no, sir, he was proud of the way he looked. He said none of the other boys had dirt on them because they didn't have to work like he did.

Judge: Did Raymond . . . like any boy in your class especially? Was he good friends with anyone?

Gerald: Just me. The other boys didn't like Ray.

Judge: Why didn't they like him?

Gerald: They were afraid of him because he was tougher than any of them.

Judge: Did Emmitt Kinds like Raymond even though he mistreated him?

Gerald: No, sir, I guess not . . . but once he told him he loved him . . . even though he was mean.

Judge: He said he loved Raymond? What did Raymond think of that?

Gerald: It made him mad. "I'll show you what mean is," he told Emmitt and he threw rocks at him every day after that.

Judge: Do you think Emmitt meant it when he said he loved Raymond?

Gerald: No, sir. It was just some of his preaching . . . that's what Ray called it: "Emmitt's preaching."

Judge: Now then, Gerald, let's go back to the day of the accidents. What happened after Emmitt refused to walk home ahead of the three of you?

Gerald: We just stood around on the side of the highway. Ray kept telling Emmitt to leave but he didn't. He didn't say anything . . . he just stood real close to Ray. The traffic passed by really fast—cars and big trucks. Our clothes fluttered in the wind. I knew it wasn't a good place to be standing but I could tell Ray wasn't going to leave until he got Emmitt to walk on ahead of us. Finally Ray said: "Here's what we're gonna do. The next Greyhound bus that passes, we'll throw rocks at the side of it. If the driver stops, we'll all swear that Emmitt did it." I think Ray was bluffing . . . trying to get Emmitt to leave but Emmitt stayed right beside Ray. So we watched for a bus but none came. I could tell Ray was getting madder and madder. Finally, Aubrey's teacher, Miss Bingham, drove by. She waved to us and I thought she might stop and tell us not to be playing near the highway, but she didn't. Lots of trucks came by, blowing up dust when they passed. So I said to Ray: "Why don't you throw gravel at a truck and blame it on Emmitt?" "Are you stupid?" he said, "Truckers are the meanest people on the road. I wouldn't want one of them stopping . . . they'd kill Emmitt and us too." So we just stood there. Every time Ray moved, Emmitt moved right with him.

That's when Ray started making fun of Emmitt's clothes. "You think you're in the army, Emmitt? Those are GI pants." Emmitt wore khaki pants every day and his mother starched and ironed them so they were as stiff as a board. They looked more like Sunday school clothes than regular school clothes. Emmitt never got them dirty or wrinkled. "You're an old woman. You got no business wearing what GIs wear." He looked over at us and I knew what he was going to say next. "What we oughta do is take his pants off. That'll teach him to hang around where he ain't wanted." Emmitt didn't say anything but he seemed to know that if he didn't leave then he wouldn't have another chance. He was standing right next to Ray on the edge of the highway. Nobody said anything for a long time. There was just the sound of the traffic and the dust it blew up from the shoulder of the road. Finally, Aubrey said he wanted to go home. And Ray said in a really mean way: "Okay, Aubrey, you go on home." But I told Aubrey to stay with me. Then Ray said: "Yeah, I think that's a real good idea . . . we'll take his pants off and throw them on the back of a truck and make him walk home in his skivvies." I thought for sure Emmitt was gonna leave then. He shifted his books from one arm to the other and Ray turned his back on him and walked off down the edge of the highway and started scooping up gravel. But then Ray said: "It'd be a shame if the girls came by and saw Emmitt in his skivvies. That'd be a real shame, Emmitt, for the girls to see what you don't have." I knew right then Emmitt wasn't going anywhere. He never said a word but I knew it. He walked over and stood right beside

Ray again, and every time Ray tried to walk away from him he walked right along with him. "I ain't kidding you, Emmitt, you gonna be walking home in your skivvies in a minute." But Emmitt just stood there holding his books under his arm. He wasn't even looking at Ray. "I want to go home," said Aubrey and before I could say anything, Ray spun around and threw a handful of gravel at us. A couple of them hit Aubrey in the face and he started crying. I would've done something then but I wouldn't have stood a chance. Ray was bigger than me . . . he was fifteen years old. I told Aubrey to stop crying. I told him everything was gonna be all right. But Ray was really mad now. He pulled at the end of his old belt and twisted his pants around to the side as far as he could get them. That's what he did when he was really mad . . . pulled at his belt like that. I knew Ray was gonna do something then. I told Aubrey to hush his crying. I was afraid Ray might come over and hit him with his fist. He hated people that cried. I guess I should have taken Aubrey on home right then but . . . but we always walked home with Ray. He wouldn't have liked it if we had left without him. Then Ray told Emmitt one last time: "Go home, Emmitt, I ain't kidding you!" But he didn't, so Ray turned around real fast and kicked his books out from under his arm. One of them landed out on the highway and Ray said: "Leave it there, Emmitt; let a car run over it." But Emmitt ran out and got it just before the next car came. A horn blew and somebody yelled at us as the car went past. Emmitt bent over and started picking up the rest of his books. Ray was always fooling with people when they were bent over. One time he pushed Eddie Litch-ford's head into the water fountain at school and chipped his front tooth. As soon as Emmitt bent over, Ray walked over and put his foot on his butt and pushed him over into the ditch. Emmitt tried to get back up but Emmitt pushed him against the bank. "I told you you'd be walking home in your skivvies if you kept on hanging around." He straddled Emmitt and sat down on his knees and tried to unbutton his pants. Emmitt put his hands down over his fly and tried to keep Ray from getting at the buttons. "Get over here and hold his arms!" Ray yelled.

Judge: And did you, Gerald?"

Gerald: We didn't have too. When Emmitt heard Ray say that, he just laid back against the bank and spread his arms out.

Judge: He submitted to Ray?

Gerald: He spread his arms out and Ray unbuttoned his pants and tried to pull them down.

Judge: Gerald, was there anything . . . anything unusual about what happened then?

Gerald: Emmitt was sitting back against the bank so that Ray couldn't get his pants down. Ray put his arms around Emmitt's waist and tried to make him stand up. He had both feet in the ditch and was leaning over pulling at him. He would pick Emmitt up but when he let go to try and get his pants down, Emmitt would fall back against the bank. He did this two or three times and each time he got Emmitt's pants down a little further. Finally, it looked like Emmitt was going to give up. Ray pulled him up again and

Emmitt kind of half-way stood up. Ray was reaching for his pants when Emmitt took Ray's head in both his hands. Ray didn't seem to know what to do, whether to go ahead and jerk Emmitt's pants down or knock his hands away. But then . . . then, before Ray could do anything, Emmitt pulled his head down and kissed him.

Judge: Emmitt kissed Raymond? What did Raymond do?

Gerald: He didn't do anything! We thought he was gonna kill Emmitt then for sure, but he didn't do anything but just look at him.

Judge: I know how difficult this is for you, Gerald, but the court must know, was there anything . . . anything unnatural that happened between them after this?

Gerald: It wasn't natural for Ray to do nothing. He didn't hit Emmitt or anything. Emmitt sat back down against the bank and Ray wiped his mouth with the back of his hand. We thought for sure he was gonna kick him, or spit on him or something. But he didn't even look mad. He just looked real surprised, like it was the first time in his life anybody had ever kissed him. He looked over at Aubrey and me. Then, he looked back at Emmitt one last time before he turned and ran. He was still wiping his lips with the back of his hand when the car hit him.

Judge: Did he run in front of the car on purpose?

Gerald: It was like he'd forgotten the road was there. He was just trying to get away from Emmitt—like he was afraid of him all of a sudden. He never even saw the car coming. There was a loud pop and his leg bent back under the car, then his back came over and hit the hood. He went flying up in the air, his leg still bent the wrong way. He landed in some bushes on top of the bank on the other side of the road. The car slowed down like it was gonna stop, then it took off. Aubrey started crying again. I couldn't see Ray but I kept watching the spot where he landed, hoping he would get up. I told Aubrey not to cry, that Ray was gonna be all right. I had forgotten about Emmitt, but then I heard him moaning. When I looked he was standing up. His pants were down on his hips but there was so much starch in them they stood up stiff on his legs. He was moaning and then he began to shake all over, like somebody had hold of him, shaking him. He did that for a while, then he walked into the highway. We thought he was going to see about Ray but when he got to the centerline, he turned and started running back toward the village. After a few steps, his pants came down around his knees and he stumbled and fell on the pavement. He got up and tried to pull his feet free, but his pants legs turned inside out and his feet were still hung in them when he started running again. "Emmitt!" I yelled. A car was coming toward him. It started blowing its horn but he ran right at it. He stumbled a couple of times but didn't fall. The car had to run off on the shoulder of the road to miss him. But another car and a tractor-trailer were coming at full speed. The second car slammed on brakes so hard it slid sideways. The truck was right behind it and it swerved to miss the car and ran up the bank just as Emmitt got to it. There was a terrible noise and the truck slowed down quickly as it climbed the bank. Emmitt was running past it when it fell. One side of the truck was up on the bank and the other wheels were in the ditch. It started to tilt over, slowly at first, then all of a sudden, it came crashing down on its side on the pavement. There was a cracking noise and a cloud of dust rose up and hid the truck. Right away we could hear them. "It's Emmitt," Aubrey said. "What happened to him?" I didn't say anything but I knew it wasn't Emmitt. It was like a thousand things squealing all at once. The dust drifted off across the field and that's when we first saw the pigs. The trailer was split open at one corner and they were trying to get out. One of them got caught in the crack where the metal was split and the others crawled over top of him, wedging him down on the sharp metal. He was bleeding and he squealed and squealed as the other pigs crawled over him. There must have been a hundred of them, all trying to get out of that one hole. They jumped onto the highway and ran off into the fields and woods. Cars were stopping all along the highway and men were running after the pigs. Nobody seemed to know what had happened. Aubrey kept saying: "Where's Emmitt? Where's Emmitt?" I knew he was under the truck but I didn't say anything. It was Ray they found first. Somebody chasing a pig yelled out and a lot of men gathered around to look. Nobody seemed to notice Aubrey and me. People were walking and running all around us but they never even looked at us. It was like what Emmitt's grandmother said about being alone. It made me afraid. I told Aubrey we'd better go home. He still didn't know what had happened. He asked if we should wait for Ray and Emmitt, but I told him no. He said: "They kissed, didn't they, Gerald?" I didn't say anything. I took his hand

and we started walking home. I guess I should have told them about Emmitt, but I didn't. When I looked back at the overturned truck I saw the trapped pig. Blood was bubbling out of his snout but he wasn't squealing anymore. I don't know what happened after that. There were sirens and flashing lights out on the highway. Daddy left in his truck and didn't come back for supper. I told Mama what had happened and she put us to bed early. I must have gone right to sleep. But later, I got up and looked out the window. It was dark but in the moonlight I could see somebody chasing a pig across our corn field. He ran alongside it and tried to grab its ears and twist it to the ground, but he tripped and the pig got away. For a moment I thought it was Ray. Chasing pigs was the kind of thing he loved. He would have chased them all night and skipped school the next day. But it wasn't him. I'd been asleep and it took me a minute to remember all that had happened and to know it couldn't be Ray.

Judge: These are the findings of this court: That Raymond Miles, son of Walter and Marion Miles, was accidentally killed by a hit-and-run driver; That Emmitt Kinds, son of John and Beatrice Kinds, panicked at the death of his schoolmate and ran into the highway where he caused a car and a tractor-trailer to wreck; That Emmitt Kinds was killed when said tractor-trailer overturned on an embankment and crushed him beneath it; That, in the opinion of the court, there is no suspicion of foul play and no cause for further investigation.

This matter is closed.

That Grand Canyon

All morning flurries had whipped about in the wind, but now the snow was falling in earnest. It laced the brown grass which bordered the road that wound down the hill past the field of junked cars to the clapboard house and the garage covered with the rusting tin signs that advertised Coca Cola, wheel bearings, and radiator stop-leak.

An old model black Buick bounced down the road and pulled into the yard in front of the house. It stopped for a moment as the gears clashed angrily. Then it moved slowly backwards into the garage.

"Can you have it fixed by tonight?" asked the black man who had been waiting inside the garage. "I sure would like to have her tonight."

Handel Irby got out of the car and rubbed his hand on the back of his neck the way he always did when talking to a customer. There were quarter moons of grease and dirt beneath his nails. He scratched his thinning hair and rubbed his neck again. He knew damn well he could fix it today. It sounded like a burnt-out wheel bearing. He could fix it in thirty minutes if it was.

"Can't do it," he said. "How the hell you think I can put another rear end in this thing today?"

"Rear end?" The black man's dark pink lips parted in a tentative smile, showing a flash of teeth. "You kidding, man?"

"Nope."

"You sure it needs a rear end?"

"Yep."

"Man, that's gonna touch my back pocket right hard."

"Sixty bucks."

"Sixty?"

"Yep."

"Man, I don't know 'bout that." The black man patted the pointy toe of his shoe on the dirt floor of the garage.

Handel stared past him at the falling snow. He hated snow. It was so damn silent you never knew when it was falling and when it wasn't.

"If you don't wanna take my word, you just drive on back where you come from and get one of those city boys to tell you. And see how much he'll charge! I told you, sixty dollars, installed. You ain't gonna find another mechanic that'll do it for that. Them city boys wouldn't even look at it for less'n a hundred."

"I know that, but . . ." The black man paused and seemed to forget what he was going to say.

"Well, it's up to you," said Handel, walking over to the stove. Every colored boy that had ever been in his garage had tried to gyp him. They all wanted something for nothing.

Just like those stray dogs that Ida had collected all her life just waiting for somebody to throw something out to them. And then, half the time they were too lazy to get off their fat bellies and eat it. He ought to kill every damn one of them.

"Well, I s'pose I'll leave her then," said the black man after a long silence.

Handel kicked open the door of the tin heater and began poking about in the fire with an iron rod.

"Don't make any difference to me. You can drive it away now and let the rear end fall out on the road, or come back next week after I fix it. It's up to you."

"When you think she'll be ready?" asked the black man, at last putting down the temptation to just drive it away and hope for the best.

"Monday or Tuesday. Soon as I find a junk I can get another rear end out of." Handel turned and looked off up the hill in front of the garage to where the mass of junked cars lay stripped and ugly in the snow.

The black man nodded and stared at Handel's back as he bent over the fire again.

"Wonder if anybody 'round here is going to town this afternoon?" he asked finally.

"If you walk out to four-sixty you can make the 'leven o'clock bus," answered Handel. He knew Marshall was going to drive in later for some parts, but why the hell should he tell him. He could catch the bus as easy as anybody else.

The black man turned and started off through the snow. Handel tossed the iron rod beneath the heater and kicked the metal door shut. He watched the dark figure as it moved up the hill past the cluttered field of stripped cars. It'd be just like a damn colored to come back wanting to borrow a car or something. They all thought they were too good to walk through a little snow.

The black man moved hurriedly up the road and disappeared over the hill, leaving Handel alone in the doorway, leaning against the hood of the Buick. He looked at the dark holes of the empty car windows on the hill. The snow accentuated their darkness and gave them the appearance of eye sockets from which the eyes have been removed. He wondered which one it was. The metal bodies all looked the same through the swirling flakes of snow. Their empty eyes all seemed to accuse him now, and he turned away, somewhat disappointed that the black man hadn't come back.

"That was my car! My car!"

He was lying beneath a car, and she was talking to his feet, which were sticking out of the other side.

"Your car, hell!"

"Well, our car, Handel. Yours and mine. You know where we were going in that car." Her voice softened. "You know what we've always planned."

He knew damn well it wasn't the car she cared about. It was that infernal trip. There was something triumphant about lying there, pretending to work and listening to her. He hoped she was looking at that goddamn calendar. He hoped she was seeing how ugly and stupid it really was.

"My two hands worked for it, and kept it running," he said, shouting up at the underside of the car. It was the first time she'd been in the garage since the year after they were married. He wished he could get out and stick the calendar in her face. Maybe things would be back the way they were then.

"Where is it, Handel?"

"All you ever did was sit in it and drive. I guess I gotta right to junk it if I want."

"You junked it, Handel? You junked it?" She was crying now, like she hadn't walked right by it on her way back from town, like she hadn't seen it rotting up on the hill with the rest of them.

He could see her feet planted in the dust, the firm, pale flesh of her legs, and the hem of her skirt. He hoped then that things would be different.

Handel walked back into the garage and kicked the side of the tin heater. That damn fire wasn't burning right at all. Marshall must have put a goddamn stick of wet wood on it before he left.

He hadn't thought much about her crying though. It was just like a woman to cry, the way she'd cried every time one of her filthy dogs didn't show up for its free meal. With twenty of them swarming about the back door he didn't see what difference one could make.

"What happened to Blackie, Handel?"

"Blackie who?"

"My dog. Blackie!"

"You got twenty Blackies out there. How the hell do I know? If shells didn't cost so much I'd shoot every damn one of them."

"And you'd never see me again, Handel Irby!" He knew she wasn't kidding about that, and afterwards, he never ventured more than an occasional kick at one or another of the mongrels. But when she stopped crying, the silence was frightening. He hadn't known she'd act that way about the car. But it wasn't the car. It was that stupid trip. And he'd known that when he stripped the old '39 Chevy, when he tore it apart piece by piece, and smashed the glass from its windows.

Marshall drove up in the truck, pulling right up to the front of the Buick and revving the motor a couple of time before cutting the ignition and getting out. He walked over to the stove and extended his hands, palms out, toward the heater.

"It's snowing!" he said. He had a young, eager face. His long blond hair was stuffed beneath a red stocking cap, but his bulbous ears loomed from either side of his head.

"Is that what it is?" replied Handel, walking over to where the boy stood. Twenty-five years Ida'd been after him to hire another mechanic, and now she wasn't a year dead and he'd gotten this: A hot-rod kid who didn't know a screwdriver from a pair of pliers, and still thought a rear end was something you sat on.

"Weather man says six inches or more," said Marshall.

"If you listen to that fool you got less sense than I thought, boy, and that ain't much. Now are you gonna get to town before the roads get slick or are you gonna wait and slide in a ditch somewhere?"

"I just wanna get warmed up," said Marshall, rubbing his hands together briskly. "Ain't no heater on that truck, you know. You sold it, remember?"

"That ain't my fault," answered Handel. If he didn't need him to run errands so much he'd fire him right now. But with Ida gone, he had to have somebody to drive to town. He damn well wasn't going there again as long as he lived.

"It'll be after twelve before I get back," said Marshall.

"So what?"

"I thought maybe you'd want me to take the truck on home and just come in Monday."

"So you can hot-rod around in it all weekend?"

Marshall didn't answer. He tucked his ears beneath the stocking cap and turned and moved toward the door.

Handel watched him walk out into the snow.

"Well, if it's a minute before twelve, you come back here. I ain't paying you four hours time this morning for nothing."

"Sure," said Marshall, putting his hand on the door handle of the truck. The wet snow flakes clung to the rough wool of his cap.

The truck left dark tracks on the road as it moved up the hill. Handel could remember the boy's smile through the icy windshield as the truck backed away from the garage. It'd be just like that jackass to throw a rod in it or something. He never did anything right.

Alone in the garage again, Handel walked around to the other side of the Buick and stared at the 1941 calendar that hung in a clear spot on the wall surrounded by a maze of frayed fan belts and used head gaskets. The first eleven months had been stripped away, but December still remained attached beneath the large color picture of a girl sitting on a rock and looking out over the vast expanse of the Grand Canyon. At the girl's feet one could see into the deep cavity all the way to the faded blue water at its bottom. It was as if the water had sliced through a million years and left this beautiful, ragged wound exposed for this one girl, sequestered from time and held forever in the fashions of the year 1941.

"This's where we're going. Soon as I get my garage in shape and can hire another mechanic."

He unrolled the picture before her slowly, revealing it to her an inch at a time. The blue sky rolled up first, and then a distant opacity that concealed the horizon and blended the sky and earth. Finally, the canyon appeared, unwinding across the picture until it reached the very feet of the young girl.

"You're talking through the top of your head, Handel Irby. You ain't ever going to get any closer to that place than you're standing right now."

"Aw, I think the '39'll get us out there, don't you?" he said.

"Huh! You can just leave me outta that, please." She was snappy like that when they were first married, but he knew she'd liked what he said. It was the kind of womanish dreaming she was fond of.

He cleared a place on the garage wall and hung the calendar that same day. It was as if he had installed a window through which he could look into another world. The rich colors of the canyon offered a vivid contrast to the rust and grease and dirt of the garage. And sometimes, he thought he could see eternity in the picture; he could see the beginning and the end, and he knew that what he was then was not what he would always be.

Handel walked back to the stove and kicked the door open again. He chunked at the dying fire with the iron rod and put two new sticks of wood in on the glowing coals. It was just like that damn jackass Marshall to go off without tending to the fire. And him complaining about no heater on the truck. He was just like a colored man, never missed a thing till it wasn't there, and then complained. If he came back today he'd put his bare ass on that stove and show him who built the fires around here.

Handel jacked up the left rear of the Buick and removed the wheel and pulled the bearing. The bearing didn't seem bad when he spun it on his finger, but he replaced it anyway and put the wheel back on. The dull roaring noise was still there when he spun the wheel around. It was just like a colored to have something else wrong. It might take him the rest of the afternoon to fix the heap of junk. It probably was the rear-end.

He tried to lower the hooks on the chain hoist so that he could hook them to the bumper and lift the entire back-end of the car. The chain refused to work properly, however, and soon became so jammed in the casing that he was forced to get a stepladder and unfasten the hoist from the metal beam above the car. He brought it down carelessly, beating the chain against the trunk of the Buick, and threw it on the work bench by the stove. The chain had run off of one of the pulleys and was tightly wedged between the casing and the side of the pulley. The hot-rod jackass didn't even know how to work a simple chain hoist that could work itself if you gave it half a chance.

Handel forced a screwdriver up into the casing and beat on it with a hammer until the plastic handle shattered and the hammer came down full force on his knuckles. Throwing the hoist to the floor, he kicked at it and stalked about the garage cursing.

On the other side of the Buick three Beagle puppies lay curled against the wall just inside the doorway. Handel cursed vehemently at them, and finally gave each of them a solid kick with the toe of his shoe, sending them flying out through the doorway into the snow. He didn't know why he hadn't killed every damn one of those curs. They ate everything they could get their teeth on, and now they wanted to turn his garage into a dog pen. He ought to throw them all in the trunk of that Buick. Half of them probably belonged to some colored man anyway.

He pulled an empty nail keg up near the stove and sat down on it and spat on his knuckles and just rubbed them. He stared at the Buick for a long time. It was just like a colored to try and fool you. Well, he'd see damn well who got fooled. He'd stuff that so full of sawdust it'd grind out two-by-fours.

He got another jack from beneath the work bench and took two blocks of wood and placed one in front of each front wheel. Lowering the one jack that he had beneath, he placed two cinderblocks just behind the rear axle on either side of the car. He worked savagely, throwing the blocks beneath the car and then crawling about on his belly in order to position them.

After placing the jacks on top of the blocks he turned the handle, first one and then the other, until the car was raised to a height for him to remove both rear wheels. He checked the bearings again, then the axle and the brake linings. Everything seemed to be in good shape.

"Goddamn snow," he said aloud, looking out the door and seeing the ground was white now. The tire tracks were gone but the red dirt of the road could still be seen through an inch of snow.

Handel looked across the trunk of the Buick to the wall where the calendar hung. His eyes moved across the first six numbers on the curled, yellow sheet and came to rest on the seventh of December, 1941.

"I hope this won't mean that you'll have to go," Ida said when they first heard the news on the radio.

"Of course I'll go. I'll go tomorrow if they'll let me." The words had come out automatically and they seemed strange to him even then, for he had never thought of leaving his garage for more than two or three hours at a time, and then, only to go to town for parts. But now, suddenly, and for no reason it seemed, he had committed himself to something halfway around the world.

The next day he drove into town and went to the post office where the men were standing in a thick, irregular line in the second floor hallway. Listening to their strained, vibrant voices he felt even more uneasy about his commitment. It seemed ridiculous that all these men should be so concerned about something that had happened in another world, and he felt awkward standing there among them. His garage, built with his own hands on the same little farm where he had always lived, and the town, which fulfilled any outside needs he had, all seemed as safe from the enemy as ever, and it seemed a foolish thing to leave what one knew in order to fight for something one cared nothing about. But though Ida would have welcomed him back without question, he knew that he could not go back to her until he fulfilled his hastily made promise. He had to prove to her that he meant the things he said.

"You're talking through the top of your head again, Handel Irby," she had told him before he left that morning. "Just like when you are talking about going to that Grand Canyon. You been talking about it for a year now, and that Chevy still ain't gone no further than town and back since we had it." He thought of the canyon again. In his mind he looked on over the girl's shoulder and felt again the aura of mystery that lurked in the length and depth of the great cavity. All that day and the next, he waited and filled out forms and answered questions, and dreamed of his ultimate task of defending the canyon against the enemy.

On the third day, they took him, along with the others, to the armory for the physical examination. There, standing in a long line of naked men they culled him, threw him out like a bad ear of corn because his feet were flat.

"Well, I'm just glad you didn't have to go," Ida said at supper that night. And seeing his bitter, dejected face, she added: "I couldn't have you going off to war. We've got to go to that Grand Canyon soon, you know."

Handel lay down on his back in the dirt and slid beneath the car. The rear end was caked with grease and dirt and he scraped it away with his fingers until he found a small crack through which the grease was oozing. That colored man had known all along. The rear end probably worked about as well as ten loose bolts in a bucket. He ought to just get out and kick the jacks out from under it and see if that helped any.

He lay in the cold dirt for a while staring up at the rear end. Then he turned his head and looked up past the side of the car where he could see the bottom two rows of the numbers on the calendar. Ida had made a real fool of herself that Christmas.

"Don't bother buying me any Christmas present, Handel. We've got to save our money for the trip."

But he no longer wanted any part of it. He no longer felt that it was his to see, or want to see. It belonged to those who fought for it, and all that belonged to him in the world was the oil-soaked ground that was covered by his garage.

More and more, he withdrew into that dirty, mechanical world. He came to have a loathing for the job which he once had chosen over farming, and his only pleasure came to lie in the total destruction of the automobiles he had once so aptly repaired. Whenever he could afford it, he would buy old junk cars and strip them of every part. Then, he would drag the shells away with the tractor and burn the upholstery from them and leave them with the others on the hill above the garage.

In this way he escaped from the fanatical plans that Ida was always proposing about the canyon. She never asked about the calendar again or came into the garage to see it, but as the years passed the dream that it had once sparked in him became an obsession with her. She talked about it continually, and sometimes she would call people on the phone for no other reason than to tell them about it. She even tried to make the plans sound immediate.

"Handel and I are going to drive out to that Grand Canyon this spring, as soon as he gets some more help in the garage."

She would smile at him over the receiver whenever he was within sight, and he would look away, and go outside again and work with new energy on whatever car he happened to be junking at the time. Or sometimes, he would go back to the garage and stare for hours at the calendar until he became so embittered that he stalked about in his small domain and cursed the thick black dust he walked in.

He often thought of tearing the calendar off the wall and burning it, but he never did. He kept it partly because he knew that Ida did not want to see it again—that she was afraid to look at it—and partly because the picture and the month and year that hung beneath it had come to feed a bitterness that grew within him.

Handel put his hands down on the ground beside him and dug the heels of his shoes into the dirt and made one jerky movement back out from under the car. As he moved again, his hand brushed against a brown and white Beagle that had curled itself in the soft dirt of the garage floor. The dog yelped and in its confusion managed to get over Handel's legs and scramble out toward the back of the car.

"You sonofabitch!" Handel drew his feet up and tried to lift the dog with his knees and trap it against the chassis, but the dog escaped and he hammered out at it with his left foot, trying to bring the heel of his shoe down on its back. He put his hands up on the chassis and raised himself a little and kicked out again. The car rocked under his weight and suddenly began to roll backwards. The jacks tilted diagonally and their bases ground into the rough cinder blocks. Handel dug his heels into the ground and pushed back against the chassis. The dirty underside of the car came down toward him like a press. Closer and closer it came, until at last he was able to stop it by digging his elbows into the ground and using both arms as braces against the monstrous press.

"You filthy cur sonofabitch," he shouted at the Beagle as it ran around the car and out into the snow.

For a moment he lay there getting his breath and staring at the underside of the car that was so close upon him. He'd damn well shoot every one of those dogs now. That would have been just dandy if one of Ida's curs had gotten him squashed underneath some colored boy's Buick.

He looked at the leaning jacks and at the blue scars their bases had cut into the cinder blocks. If those goddamn jacks would hold now till he could get out, he'd kick the sonofabitch down on its ass for good. He started to ease one hand out from under the chassis, but each time a creaking sound passed through the car making him shudder and press his elbows deeper into the dust.

He lay very still for a while and tried to imagine how the situation would end. Marshall might come back from town before twelve. The little bastard had damn well better. But he'd probably stumble over his own feet and knock the car down on him after he got there. That colored boy might get tired of waiting for the bus and come back wanting to borrow a car. It'd be just like a colored.

Through the space between the front of the car and the ground he could see the snowflakes silently piling up. Far off on the hill the hollow eyes of the junked cars stared down at him through the haze of snow. More than ever he hated the silent falling of the snow.

At times he felt sure that no one would come and that he would be left to die beneath the car. When such thoughts came to him he would draw up his knees and dig his heels into the dirt, determined to thrust his body out so that his head and shoulders would be clear before the car fell. But each time that he looked back over his head and saw the narrow space through which he had to slide, he would feel the weight of the car, like the heel of a shoe on a worm, grinding his body into the dirt, and he would stretch out flat again and wait.

By raising his head a little and looking between his feet, he could see the legs of the tin heater and the ashes that had sifted through the front draft. All about the garage he could see the faint impressions his shoes had made in the dust. His recent spittle lay drying in little dust-balls about the stove.

Near the door the pointed shape of the black man's shoes seemed so much clearer than his own more numerous footprints. He wondered how much the black man had weighed. He tried to imagine the black man's feet coming down past the car and fitting again into those pointed molds.

The fire crackled in the stove and for a moment he could almost see the shoes patting silently in the dust. But after he realized that it was only the fire, the minutes passed slowly into hours and the weight on his arms became almost unbearable. He lost track of all time. Sometimes, imagining that he had been under the car only a few minutes, he would listen intently for the sound of Marshall returning in the truck. Then, abandoning all hope of Marshall's return, he would think of how many other customers he might have on a Saturday afternoon. Everybody knew he was open, not like those half-ass city garages that took off at noon on Saturday. It wasn't unlikely that someone else would come.

The snow continued to fall. The logs in the fire cracked spasmodically and finally settled into a bed of coals that gave off no heat that could reach Handel there beneath the car. The desire to yell for help kept gripping him, although he knew there was no one within a mile to hear. He suppressed the desire for a long time, but at last he drew in a deep breath and screamed: "Help! Help! Help!" He screamed until he was exhausted, but the words only rose and disappeared like his frosty breath into the dark underside of the car. Ida could have heard him at the house if she were still alive. Twenty-five years she'd been there, day in and day out, and he hadn't needed her. And now that he did, she was dead. She probably wouldn't have come in the garage anyway. She'd probably have let him rot underneath the car before she set foot in the garage again. She'd only been in once in twenty-five years.

"Handel, we were going to drive that Chevy out to that Grand Canyon." She sobbed violently like a child. Then, suddenly, her crying stopped and he saw her feet moving toward the front of the car and out through the doorway.

She never spoke of the canyon after that. She seldom spoke at all, and inside a year, she was dead. In the weeks after the funeral, he sometimes would look at the calendar and find the girl sitting at the edge of the canyon to be Ida. Once when he had looked, the girl had disappeared altogether, and he had run to the house and looked through every room before he finally cursed himself, and Ida, and the dogs that got in his way as he walked back to the garage.

The afternoon wore on, but still no one came. Handel's arms became numb, and only a dull ache remained in them. He lifted one foot off the ground, but the feeling in his legs seemed to go no further than his ankles. They were going to freeze now, and rot off. Served the flat, worthless things right. With all his strength, he kept his trembling foot raised above the ground.

"Okay, okay, step over on this paper and put both feet down flat."

The paper was sticky on the bottom of his bare feet. He had never been naked in front of people before. But everyone was naked—everyone but the two doctors who stood before him.

"Okay, step back."

He stepped back onto the cold floor and stared down at the footprints he had made on the paper.

"Flat as last night's beer," said one of the doctors.

"Yeah," the other grunted, scribbling on the clipboard he held in the crook of his arm. "That's all for you, Irby. You can get dressed." He handed him the paper from the clipboard and pointed towards the rear of the building. "Report to that office after you're dressed."

The two doctors moved on to the next man. Handel's clothes lay in a pile behind him and he turned and began putting them on. He could feel the eyes of the other men on him as he dressed. They were still watching when he zipped up his jacket and started across the long drill floor. His shoes made hollow, echoing sounds in the quiet hall as he walked away.

Handel let his foot fall back into the dirt. The last of the heavy snowflakes floated to the ground, and a sharp slanting snow began to fall. Through the new snow the cars on the hill seemed to move closer. Their empty windows became wider and darker while the snow hid their ugly bodies. Handel stared at the exhaust pipe above him, then closed his eyes against even that.

"Handel, the Chevy has a miss in it. I suppose I'll catch the bus to town—would you look at it while I'm gone?" She was so trusting, almost tempting him. But he didn't think of junking it then.

She started off up the hill toward the main road. Then she turned, and he knew what she was going to say.

"We'll want it in good shape for the trip, Handel."

She walked away, going past the rotting cars and disappearing over a hill. The old '39 stood alone before the garage door, black and shiny, reflecting the hot July sun. He didn't even look back up the road again.

Handel drew his knees up suddenly and wedged the heels of his shoes into the dirt. With one great heave, he tried to force himself out from under the car. But the strength seemed to be frozen within his legs and his heels only wiggled through the soft ground until his knees lay flat again. The car groaned above him, and he trembled.

Toward nightfall a wind began to stir the snow, pushing it this way and that, and twisting a loose curl of it in through the garage door, scattering the glittering flakes in the dust. Then the wind ceased and night had fallen. Outside, the snow seemed to have retained some of the daylight, but in the garage everything was dark and formless. Handel's arms braced the car with no more purpose than the two iron jacks which they assisted.

Sometimes his eyelids stayed closed for long periods of time and he seemed to sleep, his only movement being the slow heaving of his chest. It was during one of these periods that the daylight failed and the darkness crept down from the underside of the car and enveloped him. He awoke with a start, looking about him but seeing only the white strip of light in the doorway.

He raised his lifeless foot again and let it drop. It seemed to drop for a long time before it finally hit the ground, the same way Ida had gone down for such an eternity before they finally pulled the straps out and shoveled the first spade-full of dirt on top of the casket. Standing there, looking down into the small cavity in the earth, it seemed that he was standing at the very edge of the canyon. He felt a strange mingling of joy and sadness, and would have stayed longer staring down after Ida, but the spades-full of dirt splattered one on top of another until there was nothing left but a mound, covered by the greens and flowers that the neighbors had sent.

Another silent hour passed. The only sounds in the darkness were the steady rhythm of his breathing, and occasionally, when he could find the strength to lift one of his legs, the clump of his lifeless foot falling back into the dust.

But then, there came another sound—the slow, padded sound of feet compressing the loose snow. Handel dropped his raised foot and listened. The footsteps were faint, but they seemed very near. He stared at the narrow strip of light in the doorway with a kind of horror and amazement.

"Ida! Ida!" His voice was a hoarse rattle that carried no further than his smoky breath.

For a moment, everything was still and quiet. Then the line of snow across the garage door quivered and burst forth, scattering its whiteness beneath the car. A large black hound slipped beneath the front bumper and shook the snow from its coat.

The dog curled itself up by one of the front wheels and lay motionless. Handel stared at the dark form whose noisy breathing broke the silence to which he had now grown accustomed. He thought of the nights he had lain beside Ida and listened to the whispering sounds of her breathing. Often he had wanted to reach out and touch her, touch her the way they'd touched in that first year before the war. But then she would murmur in her sleep and he would know that she was dreaming of the canyon again, dreaming of its quiet length and depth—its peacefulness. And he would feel the bitterness again, and would take a blanket and leave the bed and sleep in the garage among the worn parts of the junked cars.

Handel tried to raise his foot, but the muscles in his leg only trembled and fell slack. He closed his eyes again and behind his lids everything seemed to bloom with light. It seemed that he was moving along through bright sunlight. All about him a motor hummed peacefully. He recognized the sound as that of the old '39 Chevy. He took pride in its faultlessly throbbing engine. He felt the sun glinting from its black hood—and before the hood, the canyon stretching endlessly and deep.

The old Buick rolled slowly backwards, its front wheels passing the dog without disturbing its sleep. The exhaust pipe was the first thing to touch him, coming down against his face and forcing his head to one side, leaving a smear of brown rust across the bridge of his nose. His eyes popped open for an instant but closed again as the chassis pressed against his chest. The air hissed like steam from his lungs.

The hound whined in its sleep and snuggled toward the tire that was no longer beside it.

By midnight the snow had stopped and the moonlight came in through a thin haze of clouds. The blue-white light shone brilliantly on the snow and fell in a block through the open door of the garage, stretching across the hood of the Buick and along the wall of gaskets and belts, and reaching all the way to the faded canyon and the curling leaf of days that hung beneath it.

The Half-Life of Holidays

"The children were home," the wife tells our neighbor, Mr. Tarwater, "for the holidays . . ."

We have agreed to tell the truth about the children and this is not the truth.

Our children, two in number, who are hardly children anymore, visited us, briefly, during the holiday season.

"Oh, no, they couldn't stay for the New Year," my wife continues. "They're terribly busy—you know young people."

But he doesn't know young people! I want to shout. *Why remind him of those times or what might have been?*

Down the street an occasional "POP" of illegal fireworks. Kids still celebrating the New Year at noon while their hung-over parents linger in bed.

Get on with it, I want to shout.

The sun glints like a gold tooth as I swipe the hood of the Buick with a soapy rag. Weird weather for the holiday season—not really winter at all.

"We had a real tree this year," I hear the wife say, "a Fraser fir . . ."

A Balsam fir! A Balsam fir is what we had—not a Fraser.

Our neighbor, old Tarwater, is seldom seen outside, especially in winter, but there he is, chatting with the wife just the way he used to forty years ago when we first moved here. I used to tease her: What are you doing . . . flirting with that old man? Then I find out he's a grandfather. They start out young down here in the South. He sure didn't look like a grandfather. He was older than us, sure, but not grandfather-old. Hell, the first time I heard about their daughter was at the Christmas party at Tarwater's house, the first year that we lived here. Tarwater's wife told me—after she'd had a bit too much to drink—about their daughter who was pregnant and living out in Utah. I didn't tell the wife right away. I figured it was a useful bit of knowledge to have, given what else happened at the party.

The Christmas party was for the whole neighborhood—which was only about a dozen couples back then. Most of the lots were sold but only a handful of houses had been built. The wife remembers those days as a happy time—before "the tragedy." That's the way she always refers to it—"the tragedy." But it wasn't *our* tragedy, I tell her. I don't remember being so happy before it happened. I was working seven days a week—trying to get ahead, start a family. It's Tarwater she's thinking of when she thinks of those happy times.

She saw him as her glamorous hero on his big Harley with his long hair whipping in the wind.

Now look at him. He's ancient. His face is a melting Halloween mask. He scares the b'Jesus out of little kids when he's out grocery shopping.

Tarwater? What a name. Old Tarbucket I always called him—not to his face, just when I was fooling around with the wife. She thought he was James Dean, slinging that Harley of his around these country roads. He hasn't put up a Christmas tree in four decades—not since the tragedy.

I remember the party being less about Christmas and more about Tarwater and the wife kissing under the mistletoe, which was conveniently hung in a dark hallway.

I was looking for a bathroom when I caught the two of them all smooching in the darkness, though she denies that I saw anything other than a holiday peck on the cheek. She sometimes denies that there was a party. Just the other day she says to me:

"Who lives next door?"

"The Maglianos," I say.

" No," she says, "I mean on the other side."

And I say: "Oh, you know very well who lives there."

"Whoo? Hoo?" She sounds like an old hoot owl.

I say, "You don't remember your old boy friend, Tarbucket?" She smiles then but not at me, at some memory of that long ago time.

⊂⧽⊃

It was the spring after the Christmas party that Tarwater's wife and daughter and infant granddaughter—three generations— were killed at the train crossing up at Houdley's Store.

He took it pretty hard but he went on living here by himself in that big house he built. Every year he puts those old orange and blue candles in his front windows to mark the season, but lately he forgets to plug them in. His house is like the gap from a missing tooth amid the sparkling lights of the neighbors—wasting their electricity as usual.

"It's spooky to walk by there," complain the young couples that have taken over the neighborhood. "It devalues our property."

They want to "do" something about Tarwater. They ask me to join them. I'm about to say: "If any man had cause to do something about Tarwater it'd be me." Instead, I say: "Christ, Tarwater's lived here since before most of you were born. Whatda'ya mean, 'do something about him?'"

"Some people keep them up till the sixth day of the New Year," my wife is saying.

The twelve days of Christmas—what a foolish waste of electricity. Our tree came down as soon as the kids left. *Christmas is over, cut the jingle bells crap.*

"Take the car to the car wash, for heaven's sake." My wife yells to me. "You're too old to wash the car."

She's right, I'm old but I'm only reminded of it at Christmas: All that picture-taking and trying on new clothes.

That's all in the past now—long gone. And there are no toys under the tree, or underfoot anymore. No grandchildren to make a mess. And the holiday food the wife used to spend days preparing doesn't suit the kids anymore. They eat healthy. We all do—even Walker, who used to eat anything that was put on the table.

The wife reads the labels of boxes and cans and tells me when I'm having too much of a good thing. She hides the saltshaker in the cabinet.

Even that's not enough for my daughter. This year she wanted her mother to cook "Mediterranean style." For Christmas, for Christ sake! She wouldn't even put the cup of eggnog to her lips when I proposed a toast.

After we eat the two kids sprawl out on the floor and look at old photos of themselves and play at being children again. I said to no one in particular: *They ought to have children of their own.* My wife tells me later, as she cleans up their mess—I should keep my mouth shut.

⌐#⌐

"Oh, there's no place like home for the holidays," she sings to Tarwater, whose whole year is spent at home.

I don't know that he ever had any close family. In the early days there were a couple of women who visited regularly. We were led to believe they were his nieces. But they didn't look like nieces to me. I never saw them cleaning or cooking or doing anything useful. They mostly stayed just one night. They haven't been around since before he retired, which must be close to fifteen years ago.

In the early days after the accident the wife used to take food to him on a regular basis, until I put a stop to it—didn't look right, a young woman, married, going in the back door of a house where a man is living alone.

He's not grieving anymore, I told her, he can cook for himself . . . or get one of those nieces of his to cook for him.

She said I had a dirty mind. But she knew what I was talking about. We had good friends living here then and back then it really mattered what your neighbors thought of you.

"I got Samantha some antique jewelry" the wife says. She's talking about the children again.

"Al thinks it'll be a good investment some day, even if she never wears it."

That is not what I said.

I said: It's a better investment than socks and under-wear. Unless, of course, you're incontinent. It was a joke—not a recommendation to buy somebody junk jewelry for a Christmas gift.

Now she's talking about Walker:

"All Walker wants is money. He's been that way since he was a little kid."

She is suddenly close to tears. She's probably remem-bering the rejected coat she tried to give him last year.

Looks like a drug dealer's coat was what he said when he opened it. And I laughed—didn't mean to—it just came out.

"You can take it back Walker," she said. "I saved the receipt."

"Hope they'll give me cash," was what he said.

Me? I gave them each a hundred dollar bill. They said thank you, and that was that.

The balmy breeze makes it seem like the Fourth of July. I can almost smell the ocean. We used to rent a cottage at the beach every summer when the kids were little. The wife wanted to ask Tarwater to look out for our house while we were away. She wanted to give him a key. I said no thanks to that in a hurry. I didn't see any good could come from it.

I finish the hood, headlights and bumper and hose them down. My wife is still yakking with Tarwater. Suddenly my legs go all weak on me and I'm too tired to finish the car. I go into the cool of the house and rest in my La-Z-Boy with my feet up.

When the sun goes down and the chill in the January air return—as it will—I'll lay a fire in the den and we'll sit and talk of our restless young neighbors and the overflow of impolite children in the neighborhood and the house repairs I never seem to get around to doing anymore. And I'm sure at some point the talk will turn, as it always does, to old Tarbucket and his orange and blue candles—unlit and forgotten again tonight.

"He wants me to go for a ride on his Harley," the wife will tell me and I will feel the old resentment welling up inside.

Then it will slowly come to me, Tarwater hasn't got a Harley—hasn't had one in years. The wife's mind is playing tricks on her again.

"He's really a very nice man." She speaks to me from four decades ago.

I'll pretend not to hear her. And she will say as she always does:

"We really ought to have him over for dinner."

In the long silence that follows, the mantle clock will strikes six, though it's been dark, it seems, for hours.

Maybe next Christmas, I'll say.

Early Dylan

Five and Ten Cent Women

It's a warm Friday in the Spring of 1964. I am a freshman at Lynchburg College, a small, church-affiliated,
liberal arts college in Lynchburg, Virginia, a day student
working thirty hours a week at a local foundry and living
with my mother out in the country in the house where I
grew up. I dream of being a *real* student—living on campus.
In my dreams I am an actor, a scientist, a philosopher, an
athlete and a scholar, playing hours of bridge in the student
lounge, a leader in various clubs and student organizations,
listed in the annual edition of *Who's Who on American College
and University Campuses*. But I'm none of these things. I'm
all but anonymous even on our small campus—an average
student with pimples and a flattop. There's nothing wrong
with a flattop *per se*. Most of the boys who are what I want
to be have similar cuts. I look at their pictures in *Who's Who*
and in the college yearbook. I study their eyes, their facial
expressions, the shape and symmetry of their ears. They

are clean-cut, eager, confident. According to Dean Snod-grass in his address to incoming freshman, one of us could be the Eisenhower of our generation. That was two years ago. Back then I figured I had as good a chance as anybody. Now I'm having doubts. I study my reflection in the mirror. The person I see is not me, not the real me. My ears are big as bat wings and prone to redden for no reason; my eyelids droop and people snap their fingers in front of my face and shout "wake up."

Lately I've been asking myself: do I really want to be the Ike of my generation? Lately I find myself daydreaming. In my daydreams I drop out of school and head west. I let my hair grow, comb it back over my ears, wear a broad-brimmed hat and pursue my lifelong dream of being a gunslinger.

Between classes, during the little free time I have on campus, I wander about hoping to demonstrate my eagerness to be a part of this "friendly community of learning." This is another echo from freshman orientation where we were told of our school's reputation as a friendly community of learning. There's a long tradition of friendliness on our campus. Students and faculty are encouraged to speak to each other when they meet on the campus green. The older student leaders who are in charge of Freshman Week admonished us to carry on this tradition. They are very high on tradition. "Tradition is an unbroken chain," said one, "that links us to the past, binds us together, and keeps chaos at bay."

Another said: "Imagine walking across the green and being met with blank stares or averted eyes. Imagine hearing no 'hello's' or 'hi's' or 'how are you's.'"

I've tried to do my part. I've said thousands of "hello's," "hi's," and "how are you's." And thousands have been
echoed back to me, but I've made no inroads into the campus cliques. The only students who go beyond these auto-
matic salutations are the other day students that arrive in
the commuter parking lot at the same time I do. We walk
to classes together and talk. Occasionally we get together to
study for a test or an exam. Like me, they are working and
paying their own way. But most of them are older. Many
are married—some have children. They take good notes,
always do their homework, participate in class discussions,
and make good grades. They know what they want—a
degree and a better job. They have no time for acting in
plays or being student leaders. I like them well enough but
I do not want to be one of them. Lately, I've been avoiding
them. I park on the street on the other side of campus and
walk up the long hill to Hopwood Hall where most of my
classes meet.

It's Friday. My third period class, *Intro to Religion*, is meeting on the second floor of Hopwood in a front room that
overlooks the campus green. I have a window seat with an
excellent view. On the opposite side of the green is Westover Hall, the girl's dorm. Since the first warm days in March
my interest in the crew cut boys who are campus leaders has
waned, while my fascination with the inhabitants of this
Victorian mansion has blossomed. It's to them that I woof
my "hi's" and "hello's" as I lope about the campus green.

At first it was just random barking at anything in a skirt
but as the weeks pass and the sun grows warmer I become

more discriminating. I find I have a preference for the girls from up north who, for whatever reason, have been exiled to this southern town named for the brother of the man who invented lynching. These girls show little regard for tradition, or for keeping chaos at bay. They have their own rules. They speak to you if they feel like it, and if they don't, they look right through you. They stick together. They laugh a lot. And they shun the early morning classes that make up most of my schedule. The ten-minute interval between third and fourth periods provides my best opportunity to bark my greetings to them. So far I've had some success. Two of them have asked if they could bum a smoke. But all I could offer was Dentyne gum.

The end of third period is approaching. My note taking becomes even more hopelessly haphazard. A force like gravity pulls my eyes toward the window. I resist. I tell myself: student leaders don't stare out of windows during lectures—they listen and take notes. I force my pencil to the page. Dr. Snodgrass is explaining the meaning of Moses. I print the letters very clearly on the paper: M-O-S-E-S. But I am not thinking of Moses. I am thinking of Westover Hall, that Victorian cornucopia across the green that at this very moment is spilling forth its plenty into the warm sunlight.

There are not many of these north country exotics on campus—but they are easy to spot among the girls who are native to the Commonwealth—a few want-to-be debutantes, a contingent of ex-small-town beauty queens and ex-cheerleaders, and then the multitude of plain-Jane-first-in-the-family-to-attend-college girls from places just like Phoebe, the place I have always called home.

I think of the north country girls as gypsies. They are dark, with lots of hair. They paint their lips and their eyes and their nails in colors that would shock my mother. Their clothes are loose and bright and float about their bodies as they walk. The cloth ripples in the spring breeze releasing a shimmer of color like the sudden flare of a sunspot, a force so powerful that it turns my head even at the very moment when Moses commands the sea to part.

They glide down the broad steps of Westover and onto the green just as the bell rings. Class is over and all I have written is the word Moses. Did he get his people across safely? I have been both a Baptist and a Methodist in my life, attending church faithfully, and have been taught the Bible at vacation Bible schools, revivals, and youth fellow-ship groups so I know that we "believe" he did. However, in college I have learned that such events are "subject to interpretation." So it is not a given that things are always as they seem. Moses may have had his way with the water or he may not have. I'll have to check the book or ask to see one of the day student's notes. But not now!

Hurriedly I gather my things from the desk and head for the stairs, down one flight and through the outside door. I stand at the top of the high granite steps of Hopwood Hall and gather my courage. The gypsy caravan advances at its own pace, while all around it there is a frenzy of movement as students hurry to and from classes. Some are running, weaving in and out of the crowd. But the caravan moves steadily, deliberately, like the shadow of a cloud brushing over the landscape.

I search my pockets but again all I have is Dentine gum. Damn, I should have bought cigarettes. I mutter several "hello's" under my breath to be sure my voice is working. Then I walk to the center of the wide stone steps and turn to face the green. The caravan is well past the mid-point of its journey. It is time.

The steps are crowded but in my vision I am alone in my white toga—descending to greet a victorious army returning with the spoils of war—a mirage of feminine fantasies from far-off lands—virgins, concubines, geishas. I wade into the bright caravan casting "hi's" and "hello's" left and right, searching the dark faces for that one Egyptian queen with the perfect nose who —among her many charms—will whisper words of love to me in the quaint dialect of her native Brooklyn.

My best friend is a guy we all call Plunk the Monk. Or just Monk. Montgomery is his real name but in the country where we grew up everyone has a nickname. I have been called Shorty since I was three, despite the fact that I am over six feet tall. Monk, a friend from high school, is a navy corpsman recently assigned to the Naval Hospital in Washington. Since I have no social life at college and since most of my other friends from high school are already married, I sometimes go to Washington on weekends to party with Monk.

I drive north out of Lynchburg and park my 1947 Chevy under a tree in back of Skin Tanner's Body Shop in Madison Heights. The old Chevy is one of two cars I own.

The other is a '59 Chevy convertible equipped with three two-barrel carburetors on a 405-horse power engine and a floor shift with four forward gears, a combination known as "three deuces and four in the floor." In 1964, it is still commonly believed that girls are attracted to guys with fast cars, even if they have pimples and huge ears and speak in monosyllables. In the two years I have owned the ragtop I have been forced to reexamine my faith in this long-held belief that fender skirts on a Chevy Impala have a libidinous effect on teenage girls.

The '47 sedan was my grandfather's before he died. Nobody else in the family wanted it. I have vague plans to restore it, or to put a V-8 in it and race it on the modified circuit. It is a hump-backed sedan—about as ugly and old fashioned as you can get. Exhaust fumes leak through the rusted out floorboard and it sometimes jumps out of second gear when I am trying to push it up to cruising speed. Unlike the '59 it has no fins, no fender skirts, no flashy chrome. The engine doesn't rumble while I wait for a light to change. I cannot imagine any girl who would want to ride in it, but for reasons I cannot explain it has become my chariot of choice. In my mind I debate the true value of a car. Would I really want a girl who liked me for my car? The purpose of a car is that it takes you from one place to another. All the rest is just junk in your head. I've read some from Vance Packard's *Hidden Persuaders* and I'm fully aware that we can be, and probably are, manipulated by unseen forces.

I am not driving the old Chevy to Washington—I am hitchhiking. My mother's view of hitchhiking is that it is both undignified and dangerous, but my English professor, Kilkenny, frequently refers to the summer he spent hitching across the country. It made a great impression on him. He calls it his "second (other) education." While I am certainly interested in furthering my education, it has also occurred to me that it is possible that one of the gypsy girls will be driving north for the weekend in her foreign sports car that she keeps, despite the prohibition against an off-campus garage. Recognizing me as the friendly greeter from campus, she will naturally stop and give me a lift. Who knows what could happen then.

No sooner do I stick out my thumb than an old Nash Rambler slows and the driver, a young woman, looks me over. My heart does its imitation of a blow whale's mating song as she pulls onto the shoulder of the road. But is she really stopping for me? Perhaps she's having car trouble. Perhaps she needs to roll up her windows. But no, she motions to me. As I trot the few steps to the passenger side of the car I notice that one of her brake lights isn't working. I make a mental note of it. It might be a good conversation starter. It is only when the door swings open that I see them. My drumming heart sinks. There are two kids in the backseat. This is not the adventure I had in mind but the car door is already open. What can I do? Reluctantly I lean my head in.

"I swear I've *never* done this before," the driver says. "I've *never* picked up a hitchhiker in my *whole life*! But you look so . . . so *nice*."

She emphasizes some words, almost shouting them while other words come out in a whisper.

"Where you going?"

My mind scrambles for a way out. How far can she be going with two kids in the car? I'll tell her I need a ride all the way to Washington D.C. Which I do—I don't want to be stuck in the boonies somewhere.

"All the way to Washington."

I try to look disappointed but I am pleased that I have not panicked. I am ready to back away from the car, but then she shouts:

"So am *I*."

"You are?"

"Hop in," she squeals.

"All the way? You're going all the way?"

"Uh huh. It's just your *lucky* day I guess."

"Are you sure?"

"Oh *yes*. I can *tell* you're a nice person."

I look at the children. The younger one, still in diapers, is asleep on the seat, its pudgy legs girded at the thigh by tight rubber pants. The other, a boy of three or so, has his mouth around the top of a Dr. Pepper bottle. He is leaning forward, holding the bottle with both hands, his elbows on his knees. The bottle rests there, half-cocked. The dark liquid stretches the length of the bottle but it doesn't quite reach his lips. He is waiting for the car to move again so the liquid will flow into his mouth. His nose is running and his dull eyes stare down the barrel of the bottle at me as I get in. There is an odor of Lysol in the air.

"Don't worry about them," she says. "They mind good. They won't bother *us*."

The way she says "us" makes it sounds like we're a couple. I cringe.

"My name's Shelley . . . *Shelley Mae Pugh*."

"Hi."

The drumbeat of my heart has gone silent and my brain is not functioning. My body simply goes through the motions. I put my overnight bag on the floor against the front of the seat and get in.

"You can put that bag back there with the kids."

I have packed this little grip carefully for my adventure. It contains a change of underwear, a clean shirt and pants, an extra pair of socks, a razor, a toothbrush, a bottle of Old Spice, a clean handkerchief, a copy of *Letters from the Earth* by Mark Twain, and two 16-oz. cans of Old Milwaukee. The beer is cold and I have a church key in my pocket. I am hoping to share it with someone special.

"Go on," she says. "It'll give us more room up here."

I slip the bag from beneath my legs as she puts the Rambler in gear. I turn and lift it onto the seat between us.

"Mama was gonna keep 'em . . ." Shelley begins.

She turns her head to check the oncoming traffic. Through the rear window I see a pulpwood truck approaching about a half-mile away. I wait for Shelley Mae to ease the clutch out. She is still talking.

"After all, what I'm going to Washington for . . ."

She turns back to me.

" . . . well, let me just tell *you*, it *ain't no pleasure trip*."

I nod as I lower the grip to the floor in front of the bottle-sucking boy. I am reluctant to let it go. I hang over the seat hesitating with visions of baby snot trickling down on my luggage.

"I'm doing this for the family—looks like *somebody* could help out. It's no picnic driving all this ways with two kids."

I keep my hand on the handle of the grip hoping she'll talk herself out of making this journey, hoping that the little foreign sports car has not passed me by already.

She leans toward me, lowers her voice, and in a loud whisper tells me that her sister, Lucy Kay, "who's older than me—for Pete's sake," moved to Washington six months ago, having always "lived at home with Mama and Papa before, and now she's got herself in trouble." What kind of trouble she swears she is not going to tell me or *anyone else, ever.* She, Shelley, is the *only* one in the family "with any experience in these kinds of things." Estelle, the oldest, "lives in Florida, for Pete's sake," and doesn't even write home but once a year at Christmas. "She married a man who sells glue to the government and his job got transferred, "is why she's down there." And Rose Marie and Iris Lee, the twins, are still in high school "for Christ's sake, at least Iris Lee is—Rose Marie quit when she hit sixteen" (works at Craddock-Terry making shoes). That only leaves her brother, Harold, and "he's a *man*, for God's sake!"

Through the rear window I watch the truck approaching. It is still a good distance from us and Shelley seems to be waiting for it to pass. Damn! She'll probably drive 35 miles an hour the whole way.

"I ought not to complain. Mama's been good about keeping them ever since Woody, my used-to-be husband left but she caught that durn *flu* . . ."

The boy's eyes are rolling back in his head and his cheeks contract as he sucks on the bottle. I let go of the handles of my bag.

". . . the kind that makes you throw up. They call it the twenty-four hour flu, but hers started night before last and it ain't let up *one bit* . . ."

The truck is almost on us. It's empty and rolling at a good clip.

". . . nothing but green bile coming up."

Suddenly without even a glance in the mirror she pops the clutch. The old Rambler makes one violent hop throwing me partway over the seat into the face of the boy whose eyes open wide as the pop bottle slides back in his throat and his lips stretch over the widening bottleneck. The brown syrup surges into his throat and his eyes light up with panic. Foam streams from his nostrils. He struggles to pull the bottle free.

The car is filled with the scream of rubber on asphalt as the truck brakes and veers to miss us. I brace for the impact but there is only a brief silence after the squealing stops and then the sound of the truck horn screaming as the truck speeds away. I am about to breathe a sigh of relief when the bottle rams into my nose and falls to the floor.

The boy gasps for air, sucking the foam back up his nose and into his lungs. His body stiffens. He is choking. He cannot breathe. And I cannot help him. My arms are pinned under me. All I can think of is Moses. Moses in the basket among the bulrushes (his nose running freely), Moses on the mountain top looking across to the Promised Land (or is it Westover Hall?), Moses delivering the commandments (Thou shalt not hitchhike), Moses by the sea, urging me to run —run before the walls of water collapse.

I do not make it. The boy's lungs explode. The walls collapse and I am hit by a sweet rain of Dr. Pepper.

⊂⧺⊃

It is almost dark when I finally escape from Shelley's Nash Rambler. For two awful hours I have listened to the unabridged history of the Honeycup family. Shelley Pugh is a Pugh only by marriage—her maiden name is Honeycup. The saga of the Honeycups, which Shelley relates to me with a mixture of pride and disgust, is a story of inevitable decline from the glory days when her great-great-grandmother "married a Prince." "No, not a royal prince. But almost as good. Mr. Ezekiel Prince! The Princes owned half of Lynchburg back then."

Ezekiel was an old man with no family of his own when he married the pretty widow, Irene Honeycup, and moved her and her three sons into the family mansion on Diamond Hill. This, according to Shelley, should have been the point at which the Honeycups launched themselves into high society. Irene had at her disposal a carriage pulled by a team of white horses. There was a house-full of servants so she didn't have to lift a finger. "Christ's sake, she wore white gloves when she went out shopping. Imagine that!"

However, the three boys she brought with her to Diamond Hill were Honeycups through and through.

"It's always been bad luck in the Honeycup family. Those boys' father, Harold Honeycup, fell asleep on the railroad tracks and got run over by a train. *Talk about bad luck!*"

For a while it seemed the family fortunes really had changed. One by one the boys were admitted to prestigious prep schools up north. But the bad luck was still in their blood. Schools were just the beginning of the trouble, in Shelley's opinion. What followed were poor grades, pranks, accidents, injuries, questionable companions, debts and an unmentionable disease. It was just another run of bad luck to the Honeycup way of thinking.

"An education won't cure you of bad luck," was Shelly Mae's observation.

When the old Prince finally died the boys had grown to young men. One by one they had dropped out of school. They hadn't trained to do anything and bad luck continued to be their lot. But they were confident the money they would inherit would wipe out that family curse.

The Honeycup boys—one of whom was Shelley's great-grandfather, ". . . but not the one with the disease" . . . inherited the entire estate. It was to be divided equally among them, with their mother retaining a life estate in the Diamond Hill home. There were vast timberlands, stocks in the railroads, and the ownership of the city's biggest tobacco warehouse—enough money to last for generations to come. All they had to do was sit back and watch it roll in.

I was nodding off . . . then the youngest boy, the one with the disease, began having "mental problems."

"He just went off, started hearing voices and seeing things." Shelley observed matter-of-factly as I drifted into a tense sleep where I could hear words but could not connect them into a narrative.

One of the things the younger brother heard or saw was that his older brothers were conspiring to cheat him out of his share of the inheritance. He hired an attorney and soon they all had attorneys—not just one a piece, but a dozen for each brother. "Lord only knows how many suits were filed!" All the assets of the estate were frozen. "For thirteen years! You know that *had* to be bad luck." The young men grew to middle age in near poverty, living with their mother in the deteriorating old house on Diamond Hill. And when things were finally settled "the lawyers got every blamed penny."

Shelley's voice is still ringing in my head as I stand in front of the Amoco Station in Falls Church watching the Rambler as it pulls into the traffic on Arlington Pike. I am watching it because I want to be sure it is really leaving—and that it is taking the Honeycup luck with it. As the car brakes for the next stoplight I remember the bad brake light on Shelley's car and feel a twinge of guilt. Had I somehow failed to keep chaos in its place? Will Shelley and her kids be rear-ended by a semi? And will I be to blame?

Falls Church is twenty miles outside of Washington. Monk's brother, Frank, and his family live here. It is really to their house that I am going. But when I talk about these trips I never mention that. Shelley had been scornful when I told her I wanted to get out in Falls Church.

"Falls Church! I thought you were going to *Washington*—going to *party* in the *big* city."

"I am. It's just . . ."

"I don't know about Falls Church but in Washington they got a little bit of *everything*," she says wistfully.

I walk over to the phone booth. Washington does have a bit of everything. It is the only big city I've ever been in. With my friends I call it "my city" but the truth is I know very little about it. I know it is our nation's capital and that a lot of people living in Virginia drive to Washington to buy their booze. I have never stopped to look at any of the impressive monuments and statues. I know I should feel guilty about that. Unlike the school leaders I don't aspire to deliver speeches in the great halls of congress where the laws are made. I'm sure that laws need to be passed to stop people from agitating the president the way Monk did late one night as we were heading back to Falls Church. Monk had me drive by the White House. We were in my Chevy with the top down and as we drove by the front gate Monk stood up and screamed: "Hot damn, Mr. President. Where's the women?"

I was sure the Secret Service had gotten my license number, and for a week afterward I waited for the FBI to knock on the door of my mother's house and arrest me.

But later it became a part of the stories I told about our wild partying in Washington. Partying consists mostly of driving downtown and wandering from bar to bar drinking sweet mixed drinks—Old Fashioneds and Rusty Nails— that we can't buy in Lynchburg—fortifying ourselves in our quest to "get lucky," that is, to find ourselves at the end of the evening in female company.

It sounds like adventure when we tell our friends back in Lynchburg about it. And with Monk it sometimes is. Monk has "personality." He knows how to talk to girls. He can take rejection with a laugh, and sometimes at the end of the evening he does get lucky and a girl is sitting at our table, talking and laughing, beautiful in the haze of alcohol and cigarette smoke. I always hope she has a friend she will introduce me to, but if she does the friend is already sitting at another table with a guy hanging over her.

I put my bag down in the phone booth and close the folding door. I dial Frank's number. I can still hear Shelley's voice and her raw, country laugh. Several times she hints that even though it's a family crisis that brings her to Washington she wouldn't mind having a little fun "while I'm here."

Frank's wife, Elaine, answers the phone. She tells me that Monk is not there. He called earlier and told them the duty roster had been changed and he has duty at the hospital this evening. He wants me to pick him up at eleven. That means I will have to spend the evening with Frank and Elaine and there will only be a few hours to party tonight. Honeycup luck, I think. Elaine asks where I am.

I explain about hitchhiking from Lynchburg. She says she will come pick me up.

I rattle the door of the phone booth open and pick up my bag. The gas station is busy —high school boys are pumping gas, cleaning windshields, checking oil. There are two bays where cars are being serviced. A car is being lifted on a rack . . . a '59 Chevy, white with duel chrome pipes, fender skirts. It looks very much like mine, though it's not a convertible. I wonder who the owner is. I wonder if he has ever gotten lucky.

In the men's room I look at myself in the mirror. My nose is bruised and a new pimple is forming at the corner of my mouth. My clothes are damp, my skin sticky. "Dr. Pepper and baby snot," Shelley giggled as she tried to pat my face with a damp washcloth from her diaper bag.

I take a leak, drawing a bead on the pink cake of deodor-ant in the urinal, and hosing it down with a vengeance. I wash my hands and splash cold water on my face. In the mirror I see that the top of my head is knotty and that my scalp looks gray.

An hour later I've had a shower and a meal of meat loaf, gravy, peas, potatoes, pie and ice cream. I feel great. I tell Frank and Elaine—with some slight alterations—about my adventure with Shelley and her two brats, about her sisters and her great-grandmother who married a Prince and the curse of bad luck that comes from being a Hon-eycup. Elaine says there are some Honey*cutts* in her family but she'd never heard the name Honeycup. Was I sure it wasn't Honeycutt?

"Why?" I ask. "Do you want to be related to Shelley Mae Pugh?"

We laugh and the time passes quickly.

It is almost midnight when we get downtown. In Lynchburg, the sidewalks roll up after the last movie theater closes. The only business open at midnight is the Texas Tavern—a hole in the wall eatery with ten stools along a steel counter and a sign over the grill that reads: "We seat 10,000. Ten at a time." Washington at midnight is alive with people and bright lights, restaurants, bars, nightclubs, liquor stores, strip joints. We drank the Old Milwaukee's I brought from Lynchburg as we were driving in and I am feeling great, feeling lucky, as we cruise 14th street. I have a Winston hanging in the corner of my mouth. The smoke slides up my face and stings my eyes but I'm determined to give smoking a try.

Out of habit Monk rolls his window down and keeps an eye out for girls. We work like fishermen, trolling along the edge of a lake. I steer the boat and Monk works the lines. This is our standard technique for picking up girls in Lynchburg, but it doesn't work in Washington where the layout of the streets defies comprehension. Successful trolling requires several drive-by recognizance missions to evaluate the quality of the potential catch, to study the terrain, and to work up the nerve of the fishermen. In

Washington it's impossible to simply circle a block and return to the point of beginning.

There is another problem that we never experienced in Lynchburg—prostitutes. There seems to be one on every corner, swimming in the same waters as the angelfish and the rainbow trout. Sometimes it's hard for us to identify them until it's too late. They take the bait instantly and if you are inexperienced they can entangle you in your own lines.

When the night is young and promising we don't want to waste time talking to them. Later, when the bars close and the angelfish swim away to the suburbs, when Monk has cast his last best line and failure is imminent, my fatigue and longing transforms these creatures. I find myself drifting through an erotic aquarium observing their colorful flesh, their slow, sensual movements, their fins undulating like silk in the current, their gills pulsating as their lips nibble kisses on the glass that separates me from those tempting waters. It is comforting to know that they can be had merely for money, without complication or humiliation, a simple business transaction. But at that time of the night, we are usually low on funds so we leave them drifting in the blue night waters and cross the Potomac to our safe beds in Falls Church.

⌇

We park Frank and Elaine's station wagon on Q Street and walk toward 14th. The city smells of warm asphalt and decay.

"Hot stuff at twelve o'clock."

Monk and his Navy buddies speak in military jargon. Twelve o'clock is, as they say: "Not of time, but of direction." I look up. Straight ahead, at twelve o'clock, there are people standing on the sidewalk, among them are a number of girls of promising profile.

As we get closer I see that the people form a line waiting to get into a club called the Hayloft. We have never been in the Hayloft, but we have heard of it. Some of Monk's Navy buddies are regulars there. They refer to it as "the Loft."

"Look at this," says Monk. "This place is jumping. But damned if I want to wait in line. I need a drink."

A bouncer—a balding, middle-aged man with a missing front tooth—is stationed by the door. Monk walks right up to him. I hang back and look down the line of people. There are girls everywhere. Some are with guys and others are not.

"What's happening, man?" Monk greets the bouncer as if he were an old friend. The bouncer looks at him without expression and says nothing. I lean against a parking meter and try to look relaxed.

"What's the chances of getting a drink?"

"Real good," the man says slowly, "once you get in."

The door is partially open and I can see a fog of cigarette smoke mottled with colored lights. A steady hum of crowd noise escapes into the street.

"Me and my buddy here are serving our country in the armed services," says Monk, "we . . ."

"So's my mother . . ."

". . .gotta be on base in an hour," Monk says, "just want to grab a quick beer."

"Get in line . . . mother!"

There is a hint of hostility in the man's voice but Monk only laughs and shakes his head as if they are buddies just joking around. He has had only the one beer so he is not in top form.

Before he can say anything else the whine of an electric guitar cuts through the crack in the door and charges the air. People smile, snap their fingers, and some of the girls do a quick dance step or two. I find myself staring at a tall girl with dark hair down to her waist. She is not dancing but her body sways naturally to the beat. She looks up and catches me staring. She smiles and I am instantly in love.

"What we need is a drink," Monk says as we walk back to the end of the line. "Let's hit the Mirror."

The Blue Mirror, a strip joint where we often find ourselves at the end of an evening, watching a dancer named June Bow, or as the regulars call her "Jumbo."

"No way," I say as I stop at end of the line. "This is where I was meant to be."

The girl smiles in my direction again.

It is almost one o'clock and we are still waiting in the line. Monk has been to the liquor store and brought back a half-pint of whiskey in a brown paper bag and we are feeling good despite the long wait. Monk is talking to the couple in front of us. The girl tells him they are students at George Washington University. The boy, who reminds me of the faces in *Who's Who on American College and University Campuses,* starts to say something but Monk ignores him.

"My buddy's in college," Monk says to the girl, nodding toward me.

"Oh, where?" asks the girl.

I tell her and she says, "Oh."

Snobby and struck-up and a bit on the hefty side I think to myself but Monk is not deterred. With most of the half-pint of whiskey warming his blood, he is ready for action.

"Ain't a chance in hell we'll get in this place tonight," he says.

"Sooo. . . how do you explain the fact that you're in line?"

"My buddy's got the hots for a chick up there."

The girl looks me over as if I am an object.

"He may have to settle for a cold shower," she says to Monk.

"So . . . you don't think we'll get in either?"

"Oh, I'm quite sure *I'll* get in," she says smugly.

"So . . . you think you'll get lucky tonight?" Monk says with a quick wink. He is maneuvering himself as they talk so that the boyfriend is cut out of the conversation.

"Luck? Do you know what luck is?"

"Luck is a lady . . . and she smiles on me?" Monk does a quick dance-step that completes his maneuver. The girl turns to watch him and in the blink of an eye the boyfriend and I are left behind them in the line.

"Luck is mathematical probability. Do you know what that is?"

"*Probably not,*" laughs Monk.

"It is how one computes one's odds in games of chance."

"Chances are. . . I was born lucky. . ."

"Odds define luck."

". . . but now I'm just *good*."

"Good has nothing to do with it."

"O' yes, good has everything to do with it."

"You're confusing games of chance with games of skill . . ."

I look at the boyfriend's earnest face as Monk babbles words—whatever words come to him. Their meaning doesn't matter. He is making music with them and his body dances to that music and the girl follows.

"If you've got luck, you can have sh. . . I mean, dirt for brains," says Monk.

"Luck always runs out . . ." says the girl with sadness in her voice.

"Speak for yourself . . ."

"No, it's a mathematical fact."

"Facts are facts and that's fine. But the fact is—you gotta take a *chance* in order to get lucky."

The girl is silent for a moment.

"In that sense you may be right. If we always knew the odds we'd probably not play at all."

"Don't play, can't win," sings Monk. "Never waste a chance."

"Technically one can't *waste* a chance . . ."

"I can feel luck coming," Monk says softly.

The boyfriend and I look at each other. He is baffled by what is happening. I can tell that he feels some important rule is being broken.

"Do you feel it?" Monk sings on, "do you feel luck a-coming?"

"...twenty-four, twenty-five, twenty-six, twenty-seven."

The bouncer moves down the line counting off people and waving them toward the door.

"Hot damn," shouts Monk. "Here comes Lady Luck herself."

He lightly touches the girl's arm and turns her so they are facing the bouncer.

" . . . Twenty-nine," the bouncer shouts as he points to the girl.

"And thirty!" He points to Monk. "That's it! That's all! Youse other mothers can go home."

⌒#⌒

It's after 2 o'clock and we are nursing our last drinks of the evening at the bar in the Blue Mirror. On stage, June Bow, has her right arm and her left leg wrapped about a brass pole. She moves up and down on the pole like a horse on a merry-go-round, her head flung back, her black mane flowing, the gold mound of her G-string is "polishing brass" as we regulars call it. Her image is reflected to every corner of the room by the many mirrors that cover the interior walls and ceiling.

"I was that close," Monk is saying again, "that close!" He holds up his thumb and index finger to illustrate the distance but seems surprised to find the butt end of a cigarette in his hand. He takes a quick puff and stubs it out in the ashtray.

"Yeah, you had her on the line . . ."

"On the line—hell, I had her in the boat."

We are discussing the Hayloft girl and how she got away.

"If you hadn't punched her boyfriend, I'd be filleting her right now."

"She was over the weight limit, Monk."

"But she had a nice tail, didn't she?"

I sip my bourbon and take another Winston from Monk's pack and light it.

This is the fourth time we have gone over the incident— the fight—altering and creating the tale of our night's adventure in which I play the starring role. I have all but forgotten that what Monk saw happen did not really happen.

What really happened is this:

When the bouncer counted off Monk as number thirty, the last person to be admitted for the last show, neither he nor the girl hesitated. They headed straight for the door.

"Kathleen!" the boyfriend hisses in a loud whisper but the girl does not look back. He turns to the bouncer.

"Sir. Sir! Sir!"

The man finally looks his way.

"I told you, that's it for tonight."

"But . . . but they're not together!"

"Ain't my problem."

"But I'm with her. You pointed to the wrong person."

"You blaming me?"

The bouncer stops and moves toward the boyfriend.

"It's simply a mistake."

"You saying *who* made a mistake? *Me?*"

"You pointed to the wrong guy! It's not your fault."

"You're damn right!"

"I'm the one with her."

"Sure you are. You can't keep her happy, it ain't my fault."

"We can correct this," the boyfriend pleads. "Ask him."

He turns and points at me. As usual I am not prepared to become a player. I am just watching what is happening, the way a person watches a movie. Now the boyfriend wants to turn the spotlight on me.

"You were with him. I was with her. Tell him," he demands but the bouncer isn't interested in my opinion.

"Go cry to your mother," he sneers and turns and starts back to his station by the door.

But the boyfriend doesn't give up. He continues to harangue me.

"It's not right. Just tell him what happened."

I shrug my shoulders. I am not happy to be left on the street either but I can't blame Monk for getting lucky. I think of the girl with the long dark hair. Maybe if I just hang out here she will come out and find me.

"It's not right! You were with him. I was with her. Tell the truth." He has raised his voice but he is not angry. He is indignant that justice has not prevailed. His eyes plead with me to accept my responsibility to uphold the social order. It is my duty as an aspiring leader of men —as possibly the Eisenhower of my generation—just as it is my duty to greet everyone on campus with a warm smile and a hardy hello. This is the world we live in. We must keep it orderly and nice—keep chaos at bay.

I know that I am grinning because I feel the hard pimple at the corner of my mouth—feel the skin stretching over it, feel a tingle of pain that is almost pleasant.

"Go cry to your mother," I say in my best gunslinger voice.

It is true that just after I said that the boyfriend took an aggressive step toward me that proved to be his undoing, but I never thought he was going to hit me. He was merely trying to get close, the way a used car salesman does, trying to intimidate you into buying. He did not swing at me and I had no reason or desire to swing at him. What happened was simply an accident.

When he stepped toward me his foot came down on a beer bottle on the sidewalk and it rolled forward causing him to do a split. His body twisted and he fell against the brick wall face first. That's how he got the bloody nose.

I never lifted a finger until the bottle exploded when his foot jammed it into the wall. And then, I was simply ducking my head to avoid being hit by flying glass. Maybe my fists were up the way Monk described them later. If so, it was just an instinctive reaction. But as luck would have it, Monk and the girlfriend and the bouncer all turned at that precise moment and saw me savagely beating *Mr. Who's Who on American College and University Campuses.*

Kathleen is the first to arrive.

"Neanderthal," she hisses at me as she kneels and dabs a tissue on Mr. Who's Who's nose. The bouncer is next.

"You wanna spend the night in the can, sailor boy?"

Then Monk has my arm and is hustling me down the street and around a corner into an alley.

"Jesus," he said. "What did you hit him with—a bottle?"

"No," I said, "he broke the bottle when he fell . . ."

"You kidding me?

"No, I'm not . . . he stepped on the bottle."

"After you hit him with a left hook?"

"No, I . . ."

"That's not the way I saw it but it's a good story so we'll stick with it in case we get separated."

"What do you mean separated?"

"In case they call the cops. Self-defense . . . he swung at you first and you decked him. They can't arrest you for defending yourself."

"But it wasn't a fight."

Monk laughs and slaps me on the back.

"Yeah, Cassius, you put him away PDQ! . . . about five seconds into the first round."

We stand there for a while waiting for the MPs or the cops or whoever to show up. Monk says he doesn't want to leave the scene. So we stand in the alley, putting together the pieces of a legend. I quickly grow into the mythical me Monk has created—the fast-fisted, gun-slinging outlaw. I wait in the alley with Monk fully expecting a foreign sports car to slide to a dramatic stop in front of me.

It is almost two o'clock when we turn the corner and walk rapidly down 14th Street toward the Blue Mirror. Now I am beginning to feel a faint flicker of guilt trickle through my tired brain and I feel the eyes of all those earnest, big-eared boys reproaching me. I hear them saying: "All it takes for evil to triumph is for good men to do nothing." Or have people believe you did something you didn't do. They want me to confess.

So I try again to make my confession: "Monk, you don't really believe . . ."

Bong. Bong. A booming clock marks the hour.

Or perhaps it is the gavel of the Creator pounding out justice: *Too late to repent now.* Moses has been called to testify against me: "Lord, he was caught hitchhiking, bearing false witness, reeking of Dr. Pepper. Claims he slipped on baby snot and fell into the Red Sea where the whores and the communists swim. Denies he is pregnant or has an unmentionable disease . . ."

But as he has often done before, my buddy, Monk, urges me to the place where we are going.

"Hot damn!" he yells. "Hurry! We'll miss last call."

The doors of the Mirror swing open and we enter and the voice of Moses is drowned out and my soul is wiped clean as a baby's bottom and we are in a mythical kingdom where my cocky grin is ricocheting from a thousand mirrors. For that moment I'm sure I'm in Camelot where June Bow is up on stage polishing brass and Monk is pointing to the bartender's clock. In this Camelot it is always ten of two.

"Last call."

Last of the June Apples

It's fifty years since he broke into my store and emptied the cash drawer but I remembered him perfectly well. I'm ninety-three and I'm slow getting about but nothing wrong with my memory—so who he was didn't surprise me. But why was he out there knocking at my door after all these years? He's got on a suit and tie in this heat? He must be some kind of salesman . . .

It's near dark and a cloud is coming up—Lord knows we need some rain. Soon as I open the door the heat hit me—hot enough to curl my hair. Lord, ain't this been a hot summer? My light bill was ninety-eight dollars and ninety-one cents last month, I hate to think what it'll be this time. It's this air-conditioning my son put in for me on my eighty-fifth birthday. I told him he was wasting his money—I'd never turn it on—just something else to run up my bill. But nowadays I couldn't get along without it . . . heat didn't bother me when I was young but now . . .

No, Sheriff Poe, I didn't let him in . . . not right away. I just opened the door so I could see him better. I left the storm door locked. I hate leaving anybody out in this heat but these days you never know who might be knocking at your door. And that boy, he'd already robbed me once.

Heat didn't seem to bother him—not a drop of sweat on his face, his hair nicely combed and black as a crow's wing—looking like he just stepped out of my TV set. He was part foreign, you know. The Deans adopted him around the time that Herbert—that's my husband—died. That would've been nineteen and fifty. I've been alone since.

Yes, it's a long time to be alone but I can't complain. Herbert was twenty years older than me. He wanted a son. And we had one—then he had a stroke and died. Folks wanted to pity me— a young girl with a baby running a business—but there's lots of folks worse off than me. I ran the store and raised our boy pretty much by myself. I learned to get along . . .

The Deans?

Clyde and Alice Dean were loyal customers. Even after the Piggly Wiggly opened in Lynchburg they still came to the store every Friday and bought all their groceries. Not many of our neighbors did that after the war. The war changed things—nobody wanted to farm anymore. People got jobs in town and did their shopping there too. No need for a country store at every crossroads. Folks still stopped by for a soft drink or a loaf of bread or just to talk. That's what I missed most after I closed the store—the talk.

Oh no, the Deans weren't childless. They had five of their own. Why they wanted to adopt another one is beyond me—it wasn't like they had money. I carried them on the books from paycheck to paycheck but they never breathed a word about the boy to me and I waited on them every Friday evening.

They were kind of awkward around other people. They grew up over in Helltown, which is a pretty rough area as you well know. They didn't have much education but they were hard-working people. They didn't drink and they went to church on Sunday. Which is a good thing, although they were kind of touched by religion, if you know what I mean? Kind of smug about it like they already got a seat in heaven and they'll save one for you if you'll just follow them. They were peculiar that way but I figured it just came natural, considering where they came from. But that boy, he was fruit of a different tree. Now, here he is fifty years later staring at me from the other side of my storm door, looking as handsome as ever.

"Mizz Rayns?" he says. It looked like he didn't recognize me or wasn't sure who I was. "It's Dalton Dean . . ."

"Yes, I know who you are."

"You remember me?"

"I don't forget a face."

"I'm the one robbed your store."

He seemed more proud than ashamed. His smile showed a tooth that's capped with gold. At that very moment—out of nowhere—there came a streak of lightning that seemed to bounce off his tooth and light up the whole porch. I thought for sure he'd been struck dead. But the lightning didn't faze him, or the thunder. He kept on talking. I got my hearing aid in—still I can't make out what he's saying. If he's selling something he's wasting his time. I got everything I need—my great-granddaughter, she's always after me, what do I want for Christmas. I tell her— nothing—just come see me sometime.

I wait for him to finish talking so I can tell him I don't want any. What I want is to get back and finish my supper before it gets cold. I fried some June apples I'd been saving—the last ones from that tree out there—and I'm just sitting down to my supper when he knocks. You like fried apples, Sheriff? Why, I do too . . . I could eat 'em with every meal. And June apples are the best. My son gave me that tree twenty-five years ago this spring. It wouldn't have made a good switch when he brought it here and planted it. I told him—son, I'll be in my grave before that thing bears fruit. But here I am talking to you and I been eating apples off that tree for twenty years.

What kind of foreigner was he? Well, folks said they got him in Philadelphia. What I heard was his real momma was one of them displaced persons let into this country after the war. Nobody talked about who his daddy was. Some claimed he wasn't adopted at all but bought for a thousand dollars. Now I ask you—where would the Deans get a thousand dollars—they had to charge their groceries.

Some thought their church was behind it. They belonged to some off-brand church over in Dry Fork called the Tabernacle of the Son of God. Dry Fork's twenty-five miles from here, Sheriff. In my life I've been both a Baptist and a Methodist. I believe there's a Good Lord that looks after us in His own way, but I don't see why he'd want me driving twenty-five miles on Sunday when there's two perfectly good churches not a mile from here.

He was three or four when they brought him here, at least that's the age everybody thought he was. Normally news travels fast in the country—and this was country back then before all these subdivisions and the four-lane highway—but we come to find out the boy had been here a year before Mr. Owen discovered him.

The Deans lived a good way off the hard road on a piece of legatee land that some relation had bought years ago. There was a long muddy road leading down to the house. There weren't any other houses on that road so nobody much ever drove down there. Mr. Owen, being our mail carrier, drove down their road one morning to deliver a package and when he pulled up in the front yard there was Emma, the Dean's youngest child, with a boy in her arms. Emma was about seven, plenty old to take care of a baby even though she was a little slow in the head, but this was no baby but a half-grown boy, dark and hairy like a monkey and naked as a jaybird according to Mr. Owen's account. He tended to add something new with each telling, like what Emma said when he asked her where the boy came from—her answer, "Come like Jesus."

That got everybody talking. The store business picked up for a while what with everybody stopping to get the latest news of the "Monkey Messiah." That's what the smart-alecks in Phoebe called him. Trouble was, there wasn't any news—even after it was general knowledge the Deans still never spoke a word about their new child. The only place they took him was to that church in Dry Fork. From time to time someone would claim they'd seen him in the Dean's car on Sunday but nobody could say what he looked like.

For the next year he was just a shadow. Then somebody reported he was due to start school in the fall. There was all manner of made-up stories going round that summer. Some said he was a moron and the school didn't want him. What good would schooling do him? He'd just hold the other kids back. Others swore he was as black as a lump of coal and would have to go to the colored school. A few really believed he was some kind of monkey and didn't qualify for public schooling. But most of us figured the Deans would just keep him hid and that he'd never show up that first day of school.

Well, sir, he showed up all right—looking pretty-much normal. His complexion and his hair was darker than most—and he had a strange way of talking and he dressed up in his Sunday clothes to come to school—not just that first day but every day. Some folks were downright disappointed. They'd counted on the boy being some kind of freak, but he wasn't. He was clean, nicely dressed—why, he even carried a Bible with him everywhere he went. It was all pretty normal—it didn't give us much to talk about. But there was still a shock coming.

You see he didn't just carry that Bible. He could read it and preach it. A Bible-toting first grader preaching to the heathens of Phoebe—now that made a great story. It gave us a lot to talk about. And talk we did—for a while.

But things ain't new but once. Folks get used to a thing and then they don't see it anymore. That's how it was with Dalton. Having a boy who could preach better than most preachers, who could quote the Bible like a prophet, who wore his Sunday clothes every day of the week, who washed his hands and said grace before breaking bread didn't seem odd anymore. It wasn't worth talking about.

It wasn't till he was in seventh grade that folks started talking about him again. That summer he shot up like a weed. Why, he was a foot taller than the other boys in his grade. And he wasn't just tall, he was handsome too—too handsome to be a seventh grader, too smart to be a seventh grader. Some began to talk about being lied to. They figured the Deans hadn't put him in school when they were supposed to—they'd kept him out a few years—otherwise how could he be so far ahead of their children?

That spring some strange things started happening— little things that weren't that unusual except they kept on happening—cows let out of their pastures, hens that stopped laying, eggs thrown on the windshields of cars, a railroad shack burnt to the ground, fireworks exploding in a trashcan at the school. People started talking again, swearing they knew more than they did. It was an easy jump from suspecting him to blaming him for all the mischief that was going on. I'm not saying he didn't do those things—I don't know if he did or not—I only know what he did to me.

It's certainly true he changed over that summer. For starters he'd never been a boy—never been in mischief of any kind, never said a swear word. Never talked back to his teachers. His only sin was he sometimes claimed a closer kinship to the Good Lord than he should have. He still wore his Sunday clothes and carried his Bible but when he came back to school that year he was smoking and his clothes looked like he'd been sleeping in the woods. Then we heard that Mr. Branch, the principal, threatened to expel him, saying his prayers at the assembly were more about Jezebel than Jesus. Oh that boy knew that Bible well.

The break-in?

Well, to tell the truth there wasn't much to it. He pried the back window open and crawled in. I kept the folding money in the safe at night and on Sunday when the store was closed so all he got was change—nickels and dimes, maybe a few quarters, and pennies, lots of pennies. You could still buy things for a penny back then. Nowadays, folks won't bend over for a penny.

He spent the money on a pinball game at the truck stop the other side of Phoebe. They caught him that same evening walking home. All he had was a few pennies in his pocket and a pack of Lucky Strikes. But there was no doubt he was the one that had done it. He'd gone off and left his Bible in the store.

They put him in the juvenile home over at the courthouse. Then we heard he'd been sent to another state—California I think it was—where there was a new family that wanted to adopt him. Whatever happened, that was the last we saw of him. Clyde and Alice Dean never set foot in the store again, but they sent the money they owed me on the books. No, not what he stole—I never saw a penny of that.

I closed the store in nineteen and sixty-four when the state decided to make that road out there three times as big as it was when I married Herbert and moved here. That was before your time, Sheriff. You wouldn't remember it. But me . . . sometimes I wake up in the night thinking I'm in the store. I know every inch of it even in the dark—the counter where I stood and waited on customers, the cash register, the scales, the roll of brown paper that I wrapped baloney with, fatback and cheese in, the shelves behind me stacked with canned goods; in the corner the oil drum with the pump on top where I pumped many a gallon of lamp oil for folks who didn't have electricity, a show case for the candy and the Coca-Cola drink box. And the sound of voices—I hear them in my sleep—voices I haven't heard in years . . . There's still some folks round here that remember my store. But the ones did the most talking are all gone now.

No, Sheriff, it wasn't about the money.

It was about the Bible that he left in the store. He hadn't forgotten it. He'd left it there on purpose—right there on the counter, open to chapter and verse for me to see. What he wanted then was the same thing he wanted when he came here tonight. I can't quite put it in words. It was more like a feeling I had after I read that page from the Good Book that he left open for me. I knew him better than most, you see. He'd picked me out when he first started school. Why, I don't know. I wasn't at the school often—I had a store to run—but whenever I was there I would feel his eyes on me. I'd look around and there he was, staring at me. He never said anything or did anything but there was something in his stare that made me . . . well, I don't know what you call it . . . nervous I guess. I've never been the nervous type so why was I even paying attention to a little boy looking at me? No, I wasn't scared of him. He was just a boy but I knew even then he was older than his years and that he wanted something from me.

It started when the school let out for the summer, long before the break-in. I began seeing him more often—out on the highway mostly. The first time he was with his sister, Emma, hitchhiking. He'd grown so much I didn't realize it was him until I passed him. He was still wearing his Sunday suit but it looked different on him. For one thing, the sleeves and pants legs were too short. He looked like a hobo.

Another time I saw him walking down the highway with the suit coat slung over his shoulder, smoking a cigarette and looking at my store. He seemed to like four-sixty. He was on it often, hitchhiking or just walking. Of course it wasn't so big then but it was still a highway—not just local traffic—there were lots of out-of-state cars. Sometimes I got the feeling he was trying to hitch a ride as far away from Phoebe as he could get. At other times I felt he was out there just to rile me up.

I never told anybody this but before the break-in he'd appeared in my store twice. I call it "appeared" because that's the way it was. He just appeared. The first time I told myself I must've fallen asleep and dreamed it.

I hadn't had a customer for an hour or more and I guess I was nodding off when I had a feeling that I wasn't alone. I can't remember if I actually saw him with my own eyes or not. But I knew he was there.

The second time there was no doubt about it—I saw him. He was right there in the flesh. To this day I've never figured out how he got in without me knowing it. There was a bell over the door—Herbert put it up years ago. That bell rang whenever that door opened—didn't matter how slow or how careful you opened it—it rang every time. Herbert believed in that bell—he swore by it—and I guess I did too. I can't remember it ever failing, but that boy got in somehow and I never heard a thing. It's a strange feeling—thinking you're alone and all the while someone's been watching you. The first thing I heard was a sliding sound like the candy case being opened. I looked around and there he was, over behind the candy case helping himself to a Baby Ruth.

I was alone like I was most of the time—I just didn't have that many customers, especially in the middle of the afternoon. Scared is something I never wasted much time on. Lots of folks scared of snakes—I killed many a one with a hilling hoe. Dogs. Hounds. Mutts. You act scared, they'll bite you, otherwise it's just a lot of noise. As for ghosts, I never been visited by any of them so I can't judge. The closest I came to being scared was when I turned and saw him there in my store. He was standing in a yellow shaft of sunlight. At that time of day the sun comes in that back window like a spotlight and it makes the rest of the store real dark. He must've seen how surprised I was—he gave a snort like a young pig, real pleased with himself.

"How'd you get in here?" I asked.

He didn't answer. He just looked at me . . . looked at me like I was naked or something. And I felt naked, right down to my bones. I tried to move but I couldn't. He stepped around the candy case and started coming toward me with the sun pouring over him like a waterfall.

Then he disappeared. Just like that. He was gone.

That's when I lost my mind or something near to it. There seemed to be two things in my mind, all wrung together. One was Herbert right after he had his stroke— all different and confused. The other was that Bible story about Saul on the road to Damascus when he met up with Jesus and was struck down and made into Paul. I didn't know what was happening to me. Was I having a stroke or seeing a vision? Whatever it was it had me paralyzed. I just stood there looking at that sunlight. I couldn't take my eyes off it. It was quiet as a funeral. There wasn't a sound in the store, not a car passing on the highway.

Finally a cloud passed overhead and shut off the sun and the gloom of the store returned. I turned my head and peered into every corner but I didn't see him. Then I heard the crinkling of paper and there he was right in front of me, shucking the wrapper off that candy bar. He let the paper fall on the floor and held the candy out to me like a sacrament.

"This is the flesh of my body. Take. Eat." I thought I heard him say.

He lifted the Baby Ruth ever so slowly toward my mouth. I could feel the beads of sweat on my face and my eyes refused to focus. In another instant he would have me.

"You got money to pay for that?" I managed to say.

His smile became a grin. He became just a boy again. He shoved the Baby Ruth into his own mouth and took a big bite and started chewing with his mouth open.

"How you want to be paid, Mizz Rayns?" His voice suddenly high pitched and squeaky —the candy still churning in his mouth. I didn't say anything. He took another step toward me.

"You believe in me, don't you, Mizz Rayns? I can save your soul . . ."

"Five cents," I said.

"Or, I can take you to heaven . . ."

"Candy bars are five cents . . ."

He leaned closer breathing caramel and chocolate in my face.

"Money before the Kingdom of God, Mizz Rayns?"

He shook his head like he was answering for me.

"The Kingdom is solid gold, Mizz Rayns, but it wasn't built with money but with love and belief. You must love God and believe in His Son. You believe in me, don't you, Mizz Rayns?" His voice wavered up and down. He swallowed hard. "You believe don't you, Mizz Rayns?"

Again he nodded his head for me.

"Consider the ravens, for they neither sow nor reap; which have neither storehouse nor barn; and God feedeth them . . ."

His voice came at me like a roll of thunder. It sent chills down my back. He was standing in front of me—so close that his arm brushed me as he thrust what was left of the candy into his mouth. I must have been overcome by the stink of caramel. The next thing I heard was Herbert's bell clanging over the door.

They said I fainted. Well, that's a lot of nonsense. I never fainted in my life. My sister, Gladys, God rest her, could faint at the drop of a hat if there was someone around to catch her —but not me. I never had time for such foolishness. I just got overcome by the smell of that half- chewed Baby Ruth and his lips so close, grinning at me like a lunatic. That's the last thing I remember. Next thing I know Mr. Owen is standing over me with my mail in his hand, asking was I all right.

"All right? Of course I'm all right" I said. I took a look around. "Where'd he go?"

Mr. Owen told me there wasn't anybody else in the store when he came in. I started to tell him what happened but then I thought better of it. No need in giving people something to wag their tongues about.

It took me a while to convince Mr. Owen that I hadn't fainted, that I was looking for something under the counter and that's how come I was down on the floor. I told him to go on with his mail route—people will be expecting their mail I said, I'll be fine—just a weak spell come over me. Truth was, I was still shaking inside. He handed me the mail and left and I was alone again. I wasn't afraid. I was just try- ing to figure out what happened. I tried to tell myself it was just a dream, but then I spied that candy wrapper on the floor. I knew that wasn't the end of it.

That's fifty years ago. That boy's been kind of caught in my craw ever since. It wasn't like I'd been looking for him every day but it didn't faze me when I first saw him tonight. I always expected he'd be back and here he was knocking on my door in the middle of a thunderstorm. For just a second he looked disappointed that I knew who he was. Maybe he wanted to surprise me again—to scare me—or maybe I scared him—not being the young widow he was looking for but a dried up prune of a woman with this turkey neck and these little tuffs of steel wool stuck to my head. I could tell just looking at him he was nothing to be afraid of.

"Where've you been all these years?"

"Been doing God's work . . ." he said, "out in California mostly."

"I suppose they need it out there."

He smiled, showing the spark of his gold tooth again.

"I'm sure there's plenty for you to do" I said. "What you selling?"

"Selling? I'm not selling anything. I stopped . . ."

There came a loud clap of thunder that drowned him out. Then I heard him say:

" . . . make it right with you."

"Nothing wrong with me" I said. What was he up to? The thunder continued with a low rumble and he shouted over it.

"I came to pay you back, Mizz Rayns."

"For what?"

He took out his wallet.

"The money I took out of your store."

I admit I was surprised by that but I wasn't going to give him the satisfaction of showing it.

"I can get along without it" I said. "I got along without it for fifty years."

"I want you to have this." He held a hundred dollar bill to the door.

"It would mean a lot to me if you'd take it" he said.

No sir, I didn't want the money. Fifty years ago a hundred dollars might've turned my head but what do I want with money now? I'm ninety- three. I got enough to keep me in my old age, thank the Lord. Besides, he never took no hundred dollars from me—it was just some change, pennies mostly. There was something else though . . .

No sir, I don't think he was trying to trick me into opening the door. What he wanted from me was—he wanted me to believe in him.

It was getting dark outside. The lightning struck again and the lights in the house flickered. I've never been afraid of the weather myself but some people are. All of a sudden it got real dark and a shower of hail came dancing across the porch floor. I turned on the porch light but it just flashed and went out. I thought for a second the power had gone off but it was just the bulb that shot.

Yes sir, that's when I unlocked the storm door. I couldn't very well leave him out there in the dark with hail coming down. Besides, I could tell by then there was no harm in him. Whatever I had been afraid of back then was gone now. Oh I knew he was up to something but I could tell it wasn't about doing harm to me—it was something to do with his own life. Maybe he'd just got the news that his brain had a growth in it like some of these on TV. Or maybe he was just confused the way men get when they have too little to do and they get to feeling low-down and lonely. I get that way myself sometimes.

My old hand is so weak and shaky I could barely turn the latch on the storm door.

"Come on in" I said, "you'll get soaked out there."

He didn't have to be asked twice. He marched right in and looked all around like he owned the place.

"Nice house you got here, Mizz Rayns."

"State Highway Department built it for me when they took my store. It ain't much but it's comfortable, it's cool, and it's home."

"No place like home," he grinned and walked about looking like he was really interested. "I may build myself one just like it someday. It's small but it's all a person needs."

The hail stopped rattling on the roof but the rain kept falling as hard as the good Lord ever let it fall out of the heavens so I knew he was going to be here a while.

"You had any supper?"

"Just a candy bar and coffee . . ."

"I'll set a place for you. I was just starting mine when you knocked."

"It's nice of you to offer but . . ."

"I got enough food in that refrigerator to feed Cox's army. Neighbors are awfully good to me, always bringing food . . . more than I can eat."

"Good neighbors are a blessing . . ."

"You like fried apples?"

"It's a long time since I had any but . . ."

"Sit down," I said.

I got him a plate and silverware and a glass of iced tea. He was still holding that hundred-dollar bill in his hand. He had folded it in half and was hiding it in his palm. I watched him from the corner of my eye and sure enough while I was putting some more biscuits in my toaster oven I saw him slip that bill under my plate.

We ate our supper and had a real nice visit.

He said he hadn't kept up with the Deans so I told him what I knew about them—which wasn't much since I hardly ever saw them after the break-in. Curtis and Alice died within a year of each other—in nineteen and seventy-five. I read their notices in the newspaper where all the children and grandchildren were listed, except Dalton—there was no mention of him.

No. I didn't tell him that but I told him where they were buried—in that old cemetery over in Helltown. He didn't seem much interested, so it surprised me later when he told me Emma lived in Florida and that he might just head down that way since he was kind of looking for a place to settle down.

He liked talking about his preaching so that's mostly what we talked about. He said he'd been preaching since he was five years old—started in Pennsylvania, said he never had to learn to read the Bible, that when he opened it the first time the words just came to him and he knew what the Lord was asking of him. He didn't say what it was the Lord was asking, so I asked him how he ended up at the Dry Fork Tabernacle. He said it was one of the crosses he had to bear and he smiled when he added—"But they believed in me, I'll say that for them."

"It wasn't long after you left that old church burned to the ground" I said.

He said he'd heard about that too and it was a shame but there always had been a lot of the devil in that congregation.

The man had a good appetite. He ate everything I put on his plate and drank two big glasses of iced tea. Between mouthfuls he told me he had done all right in California, started a church and built a big congregation—preached on California TV every Sunday. I asked was he going back there after his trip to Florida. He said no, he couldn't go back due to some misunderstanding about money. "Money," he said, "why does a Son of God have to quibble with fools about money?"

He looked at me like I might have the answer and I knew he was remembering me—the fool demanding a nickel for a candy bar, surrendering my seat in heaven when I might have been saved by this Son of God.

"How much more are ye better than the fowls of the air?" I said to him remembering his words of fifty years ago.

He didn't say anything. He sat there like he was pondering that question: was he any better than a raven. Just then something electric went off in my ear. At first I thought it was the battery going bad in my hearing aid. But it wasn't. It was one of those little telephones that people carry around in their pockets these days. He answered it before it had a chance to ring again. It must have been something important. He got up from the table and walked into the living room and looked out the window to where his car was parked. I don't know why—but I got the feeling he was talking to someone in the car. While he was gone I took the hundred-dollar bill from under the plate and folded it up as small as I could. He'd left his phone case on the table by his plate. There was a pocket on the back and I put the bill in there. When he came back he was in a hurry.

No, he didn't seem scared or upset—just in a hurry. He put the phone in the case and slipped it in his pocket.

"I got to go," he said.

"Off to do His work?" I said.

Out popped that gold-tooth smile again. He seemed to have forgot about the raven, or maybe he just knew he was a raven, always had been and always would be. Feeding off the Lord's plenty.

"Something like that," he answered with a grin. Then, without a thank-you or a fare-the-well, he was gone. We hadn't even remembered to say a blessing—and him a preacher. I ate what was left of the fried apples before I got up from the table. I was getting ready to switch off the porch light when I heard the sirens and saw the blue lights go flashing by. I figured it was him they were after. Now you come here telling me he's wanted for killing a woman out in California. Well, I'm sorry to hear it but nothing surprises me these days. I never figured him for a murderer but who can say what a boy who can preach the Bible at six will turn out to be?

No, Sheriff, I won't tell you what chapter and verse he left for me that Sunday he broke into my store. I like to talk but there's things best left unsaid. I appreciate your concern. My neighbors look in on me every day but it's nice to know the law is looking out for me, too.

I reckon you'll ship him back to California. I never been there but if it's anything like on TV that's where he belongs. He was too smart and too handsome to be from here. Still, I'm glad I got to see him. It gives me something to talk about if anybody comes by to visit. I don't get much excitement any more—just sit here and wait for somebody to knock. Yes, Sheriff, I'll be sure to keep my doors locked—you never know what kind of vagabond is roaming up and down this highway. It's like a foreign land out there on that road. Folks complain things ain't like they used to be. Well, things ain't supposed to be like they used to be. That's why the sun comes up new every morning. I just don't worry about it. Some folks worry all the pleasure out of life.

About the Author

 Lawrence Judson Reynolds is from Concord, Virginia. He attended the University of North Carolina at Greensboro writing program in the late 60s and studied under Peter Taylor, Randall Jarrell, Allen Tate, Fred Chappell, and Robert Watson. He was a founding editor of the *Greensboro Review* and has published there and in *Cutthroat, Blackbird, Carolina Quarterly, The New Orleans Review, Christopher Street,* and *Descant.* Several of his stories were listed in the Best American Stories annual anthologies. He taught writing workshops at the Virginia Highlands Festival for many years and also taught two semesters of fiction writing at the University of Virginia in Charlottesville. He lives with his wife, Margaret, in Richmond, Virginia. He was fortunate to live in the time of Lou Crabtree, the sage of old Abingdon.

Related Titles

If you enjoyed *West of Phoebe*, you may
also enjoy other Rainbow Ridge titles.
Read more about them at *www.rainbowridgebooks.com*.

The Big Book of Near-Death Experiences
by P. M. H. Atwater

Dying to Know You: Proof of God in Near-Death Experience
by P.M.H. Atwater

Conversations with God, Book 4
by Neale Donald Walsch

God's Message to the World: You've Got Me All Wrong
by Neale Donald Walsch

Where God and Medicine Meet
by Neale Donald Walsh and Brit Cooper, M.D.

The Cosmic Internet: Explanations from the Other Side
by Frank DeMarco

Rita's World
by Frank DeMarco

Consciousness: Bridging the Gap between Conventional Science and the New Super Science of Quantum Mechanics
by Eva Herr

Messiah's Handbook: Reminders for the Advanced Soul
by Richard Bach

Inner Vegas: Creating Miracles, Abundance, and Health
by Joe Gallenberger

Liquid Luck
by Joe Gallenberger

When the Horses Whisper
by Rosalyn Berne

Waking to Beauty
by Rosalyn Berne

God Within
by Patti Conklin

Rainbow Ridge Books is distributed by Square One Publishers in Garden City Park, New York.

To contact authors and editors, peruse our titles, and see submission guidelines, please visit our website at *www.rainbowridgebooks.com*.

For orders and catalogs, please call toll-free: (877) 900-BOOK